D0065850

Lula Bell
on Geekdom,
Freakdom + the
Challenges of
Bad Hair

Lula Bell

on Geekdom, Freakdom + the Challenges of Bad Hair

C.C. Payne

AMAZON CHILDREN'S PUBLISHING

Payne

Text copyright © 2012 by C. C. Payne

Amazon Publishing

Attn: Amazon Children's Publishing
P.O. Box 400818
Las Vegas, NV 89149

www.amazon.com/amazonchildrenspublishing

Library of Congress Cataloging-in-Publication Data

Payne, C. C.
Lula Bell on geekdom, freakdom, & the challenges of bad hair / by C. C. Payne. — 1st ed.
p. cm.
Summary: Ten-year-old Lula Bell Bonner of White House, Tennessee, tries to fade into the background to avoid a bully, but after her beloved grandmother's death Lula Bell understands about letting her light shine in the darkness.
ISBN 978-0-7614-6225-5 (hardcover) — ISBN 978-0-7614-6226-2 (ebook) [1. Self-actualization (Psychology)—Fiction. 2. Grandmothers—Fiction. 3. Bullies—Fiction. 4. Middle schools—Fiction. 5. Schools—Fiction. 6. Death—Fiction. 7. Family life—Tennessee—Fiction. 8. Tennessee—Fiction.] I. Title.

PZ7.P2942Lul 2012
[Fic]—dc23

2011040128
Editor: Melanie Kroupa

Printed in the United States of America (R)
First edition
10 9 8 7 6 5 4 3 2 1

For Laurel Grace Payne,
the brightest light I've ever known

The Art of Blending In

Except for the light patter of shoes, the hallway was silent as my fifth-grade class and I headed for the school library. Then came a loud whisper.

"Pssst! Lula Bell! Lula Bell!"

My eyes darted around nervously, because . . . well, *I* am Lula Bell. Lula Bell Bonner.

As soon as Kali Keele, the girl in line behind me, heard my name in the hallway, she let out a low moo. There were a few giggles, and then came another moo from somewhere else in the line. And then another, louder moooo.

That's because kids think "Lula Bell" sounds

like a cow. I get it. *C'mon, time to milk ole Lula Bell* does have a certain ring. But I prefer to think of my name more like a brand of butter. *Try Lula Bell Bonner Butter . . . sweet, slow-churned, home style.* Either way, I figure Lula Bell Bonner is a very dairy name.

"Pssst!"

Then I saw her: Grandma Bernice, dressed in the sweat suit I consider most embarrassing—the cream-colored one with leopard print on the collar and cuffs—standing outside the principal's office, waving at me like mad.

The other kids spotted her, too. There were a few snickers.

When our eyes met, Grandma's whole face lit up with happiness, and I thought she might throw her arms open for a big hug. Instead, Grandma clasped her hands together in front of her and squeezed, like she could barely contain her excitement. "You forgot your lunch this morning, so I rushed right over with it," she said, loud and proud.

I already knew that Grandma had rushed over; her head was covered by a hot-pink scarf that was knotted under her chin. That meant she hadn't taken the pins out of her pin curls yet. (I did wonder why she'd chosen hot pink but quickly decided that once a person puts on leopard print, the question is no longer *why* but *why not?*)

I thought about mouthing *thank you* at Grandma but was afraid she might feel encouraged and go on and on. I didn't want to encourage her. So instead, I just barely nodded at her and tried to force a smile, hoping that would put an end to all the noise and flapping.

"I know how important that lunch is to you—I left it in the office," Grandma added, winking at me as if we shared a secret.

I felt my face and ears heat up—even more. My fake smile melted. I wished the rest of me could melt, too—and disappear. As it was, I lowered my head, hunched my shoulders, and skittered past Grandma Bernice as fast as I could without bumping into the boy in front of me.

(If you are the parent or grandparent of a kid in school, here's a little tip for you: don't show up at school unexpectedly. If you absolutely have to show up, then at least try not to do anything to indicate that you know your kid—for heaven's sake, don't speak to him or her. If you absolutely have to say something, make sure it's not anything private, personal, confidential, or highly classified—like the fact that lunch is important to the kid. Really, it's best if you don't talk at all. On second thought, it's best if you don't show up.)

Since (thanks to Grandma Bernice) I had a sack lunch that day like the other girls in my class always had, and since (thanks to me) I'd worn my Sassy-Brand shirt like the other girls were wearing, at lunchtime I made my way to the girls' usual table in the cafeteria. I sat down quietly next to Emilou Meriweather and hoped to blend in.

When Emilou glanced over at me, I smiled.

Emilou scooted her chair away from mine a few inches and then offered me a weak, apologetic smile.

"Did y'all see the rain boots Celia Thompson's wearing today?" Kali Keele was saying.

"Oh, I know! Sooo tacky!" Rebecca Lynn Rayburn said.

"It's not even raining!" Hannah Green said.

"Shhh! Here she comes!" Ashton Harris said.

They all pressed their lips into the same disapproving line and averted their eyes, as if to say, *We're so ashamed of you, we can't even be seen looking at you*, as Celia Thompson walked by.

I turned all the way around in my seat to get a good look at Celia's rain boots; they were red with orange and yellow flames shooting up from the soles of her feet, and honestly, I thought they were the most stylish rain boots I'd ever seen. Obviously, I was wrong. That just goes to show you that rain gear is always iffy.

That's why I only wear my rain gear to school once a year. Each year, Grandma Bernice buys me a new raincoat and rain boots—always the same bright, shiny yellow. And then, the first morning it rains, there's a big argument, which Grandma and Mama always win. As the loser of this argument, I have to leave the house wearing the raincoat and boots. On this day, the minute I get to school, I go straight to the lost and found box, where I shuck my new raincoat and boots, drop them into the box, and march off to class.

(Yes, Grandma and Mama ask about my raincoat and boots every time it rains. And I sweetly apologize for having left these items in my locker at school. Every time it rains. For an entire year. Look, I have enough trouble blending in already. I can't afford to wear screaming-sunshine yellow from head to toe.)

Well, anyway, when I turned back to face the lunch table, Kali was staring at me like I was a fat, hairy horsefly that had just landed on her perfectly white, perfectly-cut-triangle of a peanut butter and grape jelly sandwich. I tried smiling again, even though my smiles hadn't exactly produced the desired effects so far that morning. Then, feeling proud to have a sandwich from home just like everybody else—for once!—I made a show of pulling out my sandwich and unwrapping it.

Kali sniffed at the air and made a face. "Is that . . . *tuna fish?*"

I nodded, looking around at everybody else's sandwiches; they were all peanut butter and grape jelly cut into triangles, without a sliver of crust attached. *Note to self: crustless peanut butter and grape jelly triangles are the only way to go. Tuna rectangles are definitely not acceptable.*

"Gross," Kali said.

"Sorry," I said, hurrying to rewrap my sandwich before the smell could attack anybody else. I wrapped it up so tightly that the corners caved in, and my tuna square became more of a squished tuna circle.

"And speaking of gross," Kali continued in an

almost friendly voice, "remember the time you came over to my house, Lula Bell?"

My right foot began bouncing furiously under the table as I looked up and shook my head. I had never been to Kali's house.

"Yeah," Kali continued, "and my mom made chicken and dumplins for dinner, and you gagged on the dumplin's—literally *gagged* at the dinner table!—and then you told my mom how the dumplins tasted like big wet boogers. Remember?"

"How rude!" Hannah gasped.

"That's not true," I told my tuna circle before I threw it back into my lunch bag.

"You're such a little liar," Kali announced, looking at me and then turning to the other girls. "She knows it's true, every word of it."

It was true. Only, it was *Kali* who had come to my house, *Kali* who'd gagged, and *Kali* who'd compared dumplins to big wet boogers when my mama had made chicken and dumplins for supper.

I opened my mouth to say so but snapped it shut once I got a good look at all the girls staring at me. They all believed Kali, even Emilou—I could tell—and somehow, I knew there wasn't anything I could say to change their minds. It was clear that

Kali knew it, too, the way she sat there so confident, so absolutely sure of herself, smiling a mean little smile at me. So, I grabbed my lunch and stood up.

"And that's not all," Kali said. "You won't believe what she . . ."

I hurried away so I wouldn't have to hear what came next. If there was nothing I could do about it, I didn't want to hear it. Honestly, I didn't want to hear it no matter what.

I plopped down two tables over, next to Alan West and his friends from Miss Cousins's class, Richard Smith and Bill Leavey. Alan looked way too happy to see me—like Grandma Bernice had looked when she'd spotted me in the hallway this morning.

Ignoring Alan and Richard and Bill, I unpacked my lunch—except for the smushed sandwich. The last item I pulled from my lunch bag was a banana, and apparently, this was a downright magical moment for the three of them.

Alan lifted the banana from his own lunch tray and waved it at me, as if liking bananas would instantly and permanently bind us.

I nodded, hoping Alan would put his banana down. He didn't.

Richard immediately pulled a banana out of his lunchbox and announced, "I call this pure potassium."

Alan lifted his banana to his mouth like a microphone and said in his best Alex Trebek from *Jeopardy!* voice, "Oh, I'm sorry, Richard, that's incorrect. In addition to potassium, bananas also contain magnesium, phosphorus, calcium, sodium, iron, selenium, manganese, copper, zinc, and three kinds of sugars. Not to mention fiber."

He'd barely finished when Bill spoke into his banana, "I'll take fruits for six hundred, Alex. This fruit can help reduce the symptoms of stress and depression, can help improve eyesight and digestion, and can help to prevent certain cancers, kidney problems, high blood pressure, and anemia. What are bananas?"

"I would be remiss if I didn't point out," Alan/Alex responded in his most condescending voice, "that bananas can be classified as fruits, herbs, or berries because—"

"I hate *Jeopardy!*" I mumbled, rolling my eyes and shoving my entire lunch back into its sack, banana first.

The table fell silent. When I looked up, Alan,

Richard, and Bill were all gaping at me as if I'd said I hated America, or worse, *Star Wars*. They all lived for *Star Wars*. And *Jeopardy!* too, I guess.

But the silence didn't last long. After that, they all argued passionately over the proper scientific classification of bananas.

Meanwhile, I just sat there with my chin propped on my hands until we were finally excused from the cafeteria. I didn't listen and I didn't talk, because I don't care about bananas that much. And I didn't eat, because no matter how bad it is, I prefer a hot lunch—or no lunch—to a cold lunch. Granted, I would've been willing to eat a cold lunch every single day if it meant fitting in with the other girls. But bringing my lunch hadn't helped me one bit.

As I sat there, I remembered Kali tasting Mama's dumplins back when we were in the third grade, back when Kali and I were actually friends. To be fair, I have to say that Kali was upset that night. It was, after all, her first time visiting my house, and she'd been on her very best behavior; she'd wanted Mama and Grandma Bernice to like her—*especially* Grandma Bernice, I could tell. And then the first bite of food she put in her mouth—a dumplin— had caused Kali to gag and cough until tears ran from her eyes. Honestly, I thought she was going to throw up right there at the supper table—I think Kali thought so, too. Once she spit the dumplin out and got control of herself, she continued to cry a little, and that's when she blurted out the bit about dumplins tasting like big wet boogers. I don't think she meant to insult anybody but to explain herself—she seemed embarrassed. I wasn't mad at her at the time. No one was. We all felt sorry that we'd made Kali gag and cry.

After that, Grandma Bernice ran down a list of things she could make for Kali "in a jiffy." It took a lot of encouraging, but finally Kali admitted that she liked peanut butter. So, Grandma got up and fixed Kali a peanut butter and grape jelly sandwich cut into triangles, without crusts. Kali had thanked her over and over again, and I remember thinking, *What's the big deal?*

My thoughts drifted from chicken and dumplins and PB&J sandwiches of the past to the day's tuna fish. *What kind of idiot brings tuna?* I asked myself. Might as well have brought a can of stinky sardines and shown the other girls how their little heads were ripped clean off their little bodies. Idiot.

I should've known better. See, blending in at

C. C. Payne

school is a very delicate art form. For starters, it requires the right lunch, the right clothes, the right friends, and relatives who don't show up unexpectedly. And I had none of those things.

Tuna versus PB&J

Under the best circumstances, Alan West's hair is a dark mass of super-tight curls, all of which seem to be trying to escape from his head to lead a life of their own—which they are already doing, if you ask me. If his curls could talk, I'm pretty sure they'd say things like *kapow!* or *shazam!*

That evening, Alan's house did *not* offer the best circumstances; the humidifier and fan that Alan and I were using to create mini-tornados for our science project had really done a number on Alan's hair. It had doubled in size and curl-craziness. His hair, in addition to his extreme excitement over our tornados, made me think, *Mad scientist, post-elec-trocution.* Plus, the small, circular, white-ish scar on Alan's left cheek—which I normally didn't notice—somehow made him look the part even more.

When Mrs. West came into the kitchen, she gasped and latched onto the doorframe with both hands as she rocked back on her heels. I didn't know if she'd been startled by the tiny twister on her kitchen table or by the ginormous head of hair on her son's head—but I'm betting it was the hair.

Alan didn't notice. He was too busy moving the fan around, causing our tornado to dance like a marionette under his mad-scientist control. "Look! Look!"

"Yes, I . . . I see." Mrs. West took a couple of deep breaths, dropped her arms at her sides, and said, "Remember, Lula Bell still has a piano and voice lesson tonight," without ever taking her eyes off Alan's hair.

Alan frowned, set the fan down, and switched it off. "Okay, okay, we're finished," he said, as if Mrs. West had reminded us of my music lesson sixteen times, which she hadn't. That was our first reminder.

"Maybe we could just catch up on my music lessons next week," I suggested helpfully.

Mrs. West checked her watch. "It has been a long day, and I know you must be tired, Lula Bell."

"Yes, ma'am," I said, trying to look droopy.

"I understand," Mrs. West said, giving my arm a little pat.

"Thank you," I said, feeling myself droop even more as relief spread through me. I began gathering up my things and stuffing them into my backpack.

"I understand," Mrs. West said again, "and I'm sorry . . . but Lula Bell, the show *must* go on!"

I stopped moving and sighed. I knew this meant that we were going ahead with my music lesson no matter how tired I was, no matter how late it was, no matter what.

Okay, okay, I wasn't that tired and it wasn't that late—only a little past nine o'clock. But even so, as I dialed our house, I had to wonder if Grandma Bernice was still awake. Grandma Bernice went to bed at nine every night and got up at five every morning, like clockwork. She said it was just the way she was made.

Now, I knew that Grandma Bernice wouldn't go to bed until everyone was home, but I also knew that she sometimes fell asleep accidentally, which is what I thought must've happened as I listened to the phone ringing, ringing, ringing in my ear. I could just picture Grandma, feet up, head back, mouth hanging open, snoring away in the poofy recliner she called her "lazy-girl chair."

Suddenly, Grandma Bernice's voice cut in. "Hello?"

"Were you sleeping?" I asked, turning away from Alan in a small attempt at privacy.

"'Course not!" Grandma Bernice was quick to say. "I was just resting my eyes is all." (According to Grandma Bernice, she is never asleep in her lazy-girl chair; she is only resting her eyes. And she doesn't snore either. Not ever.)

"I'm going to be late," I said.

Grandma said the same thing she always said under these circumstances: "I'll be right here waiting for you."

"And you'll do this waiting . . . um, *awake*, right?"

"I'll be awake," Grandma promised.

I put the phone back, and when I turned around, Alan was standing in front of the refrigerator, drinking a Yoo-hoo. He gave me a goofy grin.

"You should look in a mirror," I said on my way out of the kitchen.

Alan's grin slipped just a little.

Throughout my music lesson, I half-waited for the terrorized screams I thought Alan's reflection deserved. But they never came.

I'd just pulled my hands back from the piano keys, having finished playing and singing my song for the last time, when Alan began clapping from his usual spying position at the top of the stairs. I meant to give him a dirty look, but when my eyes landed on him, I couldn't help smiling. Alan had tried to fix his hair—how, I didn't know—maybe just by brushing it. The result was an explosive afro with the added bonus of static cling. His hair no longer merely said *shazam!* but *SHAZAYAM, BABY!*

Alan smiled back, stood, and trotted down the stairs to see me out, like he always did. "Good work on our science project," he said when we reached his front door.

"You, too," I said, and I meant it.

Alan and I made pretty good partners. We were both smart, did our fair share of the work, and hoped to earn a good grade. The problem was that Alan didn't care who knew this. I did. I didn't want anybody thinking of me as especially smart, because "smart" wouldn't help me fit in. Which is why I would've gladly traded my partnership with Alan for a partnership with almost anybody else, even if it meant doing all the work by myself.

Alan was like tuna when I really needed PB&J.

Paparazzi and Other Problems

I sprinted past the three houses separating the Wests' house from our house and cut around back, hoping with all my heart that Grandma was still awake.

She was. When I burst through the back door, Grandma Bernice was sitting at the kitchen table, carefully cutting fabric into little squares that were the beginning of a quilt. She was wearing her bootie-slippers along with her soft pink bathrobe that zipped up the front. Her wavy white hair was littered with black bobby pins.

Grandma's eyes sparked with happiness, and she smiled when she saw me. "Well, well, well, if it isn't Lula Bell! How'd your music lesson go?"

For a few seconds, I just stood there panting. Then I announced, "I wish Alan would stop spying on me (pant, pant). I always feel like (pant) I've been caught singing into my hairbrush in the bathroom mirror (pant, pant)."

"You just keep right on singin', honey."

I peeled off my sweatshirt, and as I did, Grandma got up singing her favorite song of all time: "This little light of mine, I'm gonna let it shine . . ."

I used my toes to pry my sneakers off while Grandma opened the refrigerator. "You've got to be willin' to let your light shine no matter who's watchin'—if you let *your* light shine, then others will feel better about letting *their* lights shine, and we all have a light in us that wants to shine, that's meant to shine. You understand?"

I thought about how I had never once seen light shine from a person and how if I ever did see a shiny person, my first question wouldn't be, "Hey, how do I let my light shine?" It would be, "What planet are you from?"

"Lula Bell? Do you understand?"

"Yes, ma'am," I said, even though I had no idea what Grandma was talking about. I picked up my sneakers and tossed them into the shoe basket by the back door.

"I'm sorry if I embarrassed you at school this morning," Grandma Bernice said, her back still to me.

I froze. "Oh . . . um . . . no, ma'am—you didn't."

Grandma Bernice gave me a quick glance over her shoulder, and that was enough. I knew that we both knew I was lying.

Knowing that Grandma knew I'd felt ashamed of her made my heart squeezy and my stomach queasy. But what could I do? I'd already tried telling her I wasn't embarrassed. She knew better. So I stood there, fidgeting with the pinky-finger-size hole inside my left pocket.

"Well, anyhoo, how'd it go—with the lunch, I mean. Were you able to sit with Emilou and the other girls?"

"Yes, ma'am . . . no, ma'am—not really—I tried, but. . . ." I shrugged.

"Aw, I'm sorry—and you wore your Snotty-Brand shirt and everything!"

"*Sassy*-Brand," I corrected. "And my shirt was fine. My lunch was the problem—I made the wrong lunch."

"Oh," Grandma said. "What's the right lunch?"

"Peanut butter and grape jelly cut into triangles with no crusts."

"But, Lula Bell, you don't even like peanut butter."

"Lunch isn't about *eating*," I informed her.

"Well, *this* is." Grandma returned to the table and set out a small glass of milk for me, along with one of her world-famous, blue-ribbon, homemade, deep-fried, triple-dipped, glazed doughnuts, with extra icing.

I smiled so big that I actually felt my ears move, because Grandma Bernice's doughnuts were the best thing I'd ever put in my mouth. *The best thing.* Ever.

Grandma smiled back.

"What's the occasion?" I asked then, because Grandma Bernice's doughnuts were like a reward in our house; they meant a job well done.

"Your report card—good job!" Grandma said as she sat down and nudged her glasses back up on her nose. "Oh, and your mama reached her sales goal in hair products. I told her there'd be doughnuts waiting whenever she gets home from the beauty shop, so you can't eat 'em all."

I nodded. "Thank you."

"You're welcome." Grandma gathered up the fabric squares and stuffed everything back into her quilting basket.

I eyed the *White House Watch* on the kitchen counter.

The *White House Watch* is the weekly newspaper in small-town White House, Tennessee, where we live. No, *the* White House isn't here (it's in Washington, D.C.) and no, not all the houses here are white. The city of White House is named after a white clapboard house that served as an inn for people traveling between Kentucky and Nashville, Tennessee, back in 1829. That inn is now the town library and a museum, too. So the building is for readers and non-readers alike, which I think is very thoughtful of the library people.

Come to think of it, all the business people in White House are thoughtful like that—they all offer something for everyone. The gas station is also a deli and a bakery; the movie rental store is also a tanning salon, with all kinds of lotions and potions for sale; the photographer's studio sells furniture on the weekends, and then there's the restaurant/ice cream parlor/arcade. My favorite is the florist's shop because they sell the cutest jewelry and flip-flops.

But the newspaper just puts out the newspaper and nothing else. It arrives in our mailbox every Thursday morning, like clockwork. And by the time I get home on Thursday nights, Grandma Bernice has shopped the obituaries and decided how she would most like to die that week.

Look, "death is part of life," Grandma Bernice always says.

I picked up the newspaper and flipped to the obituaries. "So? What's it going to be? Deadly police chase? Grizzly bear attack?"

No matter that no one ever died of anything exciting here in our little town. In fact, most of the obituaries didn't even tell *how* the person died; they just said when they died and who survived them, and gave information about the funeral. It was these mystery obits that really inspired Grandma and me to be creative.

"You'll never guess it. *Never*," Grandma said with a twinkle in her blue eyes. "But try."

I stood completely still and tried to think of something I would never guess. I thought and thought. The only sound in the house was that of the toilet running in the hallway bathroom—it never stops. I thought some more.

Finally, I came up with, "Explosive diarrhea?"

"Lula!" Grandma started, appalled. Then she covered her mouth . . . and began to shake all over. She was laughing!

I laughed, too.

When we started to calm down, I asked, "Does it have anything to do with gazelles?" because last week Grandma Bernice had said that she would like to be mistaken for a gazelle and shot by a hunter's bow and arrow. (There was definitely nothing gazelle-like about Grandma Bernice.)

"Nope, no gazelles."

"Hmmm. Attacked by a hippopotamus in Old Hickory Lake?" I said, making a swimming motion with my arms and then pretending to be dragged underwater by something unseen. I shrieked and coughed and gasped and then finally lay still on the linoleum, playing dead. After a few seconds I twitched, turned my head toward Grandma, fixed my eyes, and let my tongue loll out of my mouth.

Grandma Bernice giggled. "Nope."

I sat up and thought some more. "Eaten by a great white shark while surfing in the Cumberland River?" I had water on the brain now.

No matter that gazelles and hippos only lived

in Africa, and the closest sharks were probably off the coast of Alabama or Florida. Accuracy wasn't the point of this game; fun was.

"You'll never guess it," Grandma said again, pleased with herself.

I got up off the floor and took my place at the kitchen table, across from Grandma Bernice. "Then tell me," I said, picking up my doughnut.

"You know, Eula Beth Wilks died late Sunday night," Grandma said.

Eula Beth Wilks had been in my grandma's Sunday school class at church.

"No, I didn't know," I said once I'd swallowed. "I'm sorry, Grandma."

Grandma Bernice shrugged. "Part of life."

"What did Mrs. Wilks die of?"

"Old age—she died in her sleep," Grandma said matter-of-factly. "I saw her at church on Sunday morning. She was fine . . . happy, excited."

"How come?" I asked.

"Eula Beth's whole family was coming to her house for lunch after church."

I nodded and chewed.

"And I've decided that's exactly how I'd like to go," Grandma said.

My eyes bulged. "In your sleep? But that's so boring!"

Grandma leaned over the table like she was about to tell me a secret and said, "Yes, but I'm tellin' you, Lula Bell, it really is the way to go—peaceful and warm in your own bed, having been surrounded by those you love."

I didn't consider this to be Grandma Bernice's best work. Not even close. "Well, um, okay," I said, trying not to sound disappointed. I didn't have to try too hard; it was almost impossible to feel disappointment while eating one of Grandma Bernice's doughnuts.

"Eula Beth almost died on her birthday," Grandma pointed out. "I think it's nice when a person dies on the same day they were born. It gives the impression that things went exactly as planned—it's just so . . . elegant."

"Yeah, elegant," I said with a mouth full of doughnut. No way did I want to die on my birthday. Then I wouldn't have time to enjoy my presents!

"Make sure it says both my date of birth and my date of death on my headstone, will you, Lula Bell?"

I nodded.

"And you?" Grandma said, leaning back in her chair.

That was the moment I'd been waiting for. I swallowed, sat up straight, and proudly announced, "I'd like to be crushed to death by a mob of adoring fans and paparazzi. Then, the next day, the newspaper headlines will read 'International Superstar Lula Bell Bonner Loved to Death—Literally.'"

"Excellent," Grandma said with real appreciation, just before her whole face twisted up. Her mouth puckered, her nose bunched, her eyes and forehead scrunched together, and wrinkles appeared—everywhere. This was how Grandma Bernice pushed her glasses up on her nose using her face instead of her hands. (Also, sometimes, all this squinchy-face action caused Grandma's dentures to knock around inside her mouth, which always embarrassed me in front of other people.) It was not an attractive habit, as I'd recently pointed out—as politely as possible. Ever since then, Grandma Bernice had been trying to stop. She'd made me promise to tell her whenever she did it.

"Gotcha!" I said, pointing a finger at her. "You just did it again!"

Grandma's hands clenched. "Oh poopoopahduke! You're right!"

"Poopoopahduke" was Grandma Bernice's version of "darn" or "shoot." I once asked her where she learned that and she said, "Oh, you know, it's a saying." (Here's a little tip for you: it's not a saying if nobody else says it.)

"All right, you got me this time. But it's not going to happen again." Grandma seemed to settle herself.

"Anyway," I said, "after my death, the paparazzi will descend on my hometown to cover the local reaction to my tragic death."

"I hadn't thought of that, but you're right. This place'll be swarming with news helicopters and vans, journalists, photographers, lights, and cameras!" Grandma Bernice said.

"And all my friends—by then, I'll have lots of friends—will cry their eyes out on TV and say how they always knew I was destined for stardom."

"You are so right, Lula Bell! And it all starts with the fifth grade talent show—I can hardly wait!"

Oh. Here I thought we were just kidding around, but the look on Grandma's face made it clear she wasn't kidding around about that talent show—not one little bit.

I ignored Grandma, put on a sad face, and tried to change the subject. "After I'm dead, Kali Keele is sure going to be sorry about the way she treated me."

"She'll feel terrible," Grandma agreed. "Kali probably won't even get to be on TV!"

I almost smiled at that but caught myself. Now wasn't a time for smiling. Now was when we pretended to feel sorry for all the people who'd have to carry big, heaping loads of guilt following our tragic and untimely deaths.

"And after I die in my sleep," Grandma said, "Alyssa Bolgery will feel just awful about the way she pushed ahead of me in Al's Food Valu yesterday."

"She will," I said, shaking my head sadly. "She'll never forgive herself."

"And to think, I've been praying for Alyssa and her mama every night for weeks!" Grandma Bernice added.

I wasn't overly impressed by Grandma's prayers. Not only does everybody know everybody here, but everybody knows everybody else's business. Business gets passed around in the form of prayer requests; for example: "Bernice, did you hear about poor Shug McFee? No? Well, you need to start praying for him 'cause he done fallen off the wagon and started drinking again, and Lyla Langford heard from Carol Shaeffer who heard from Judy Hibbard who heard *straight* from Shug's next-door neighbor that his wife is ready to throw him out of the house!" To which, Grandma Bernice always replies, "Oh, I will! I'll start praying right away!" As much as I hear this kind of stuff, well . . . I'm pretty sure that everybody's always praying for everybody here. So I figure Grandma Bernice was only one of about eight thousand people praying for Alyssa and her mama—whatever their problem was.

We heard the garage door then. Grandma and I both zipped our lips just in time, as Mama clacked into the kitchen lugging her big black purse. With effort, she hefted her purse onto the kitchen counter. (My mama carries the biggest purse I've ever seen. It has all the usual stuff in it, plus pepper spray, Germ-X, Band-Aids, Neosporin, an extra cell phone battery, her favorite hair-cutting scissors in a special leather case, her appointment book, and Dentyne gum. What can I tell you? I guess if my mama were attacked, she could fend off her attacker with pepper spray, call the police, wash her hands, treat her own wounds, give haircuts while she waited for the police to arrive, and book appointments for all those she couldn't get to—all without ever having to worry about bad breath.)

A little piece of fabric peeking out of Grandma Bernice's quilting basket caught Mama's eye right away. "Mother, you didn't buy *more* material today, did you?"

"Just a little," Grandma hurried to explain. "There was a remnant sale over at Jo-Ann's Fabrics—it was practically free!"

Mama closed her eyes and took a deep breath, like she was trying very hard to hold on to what was left of her patience. Then she opened her eyes, blinked, and said, "You're never going to be able to make use of all that fabric. You should give some away. And for goodness sake, stop buying it!"

Grandma Bernice let out an angry little "Hmph!" It was her way of having the last word whenever she couldn't think of one.

For a minute Mama just stood there, studying Grandma Bernice and me. Then she said, "You two were doing it again, weren't you?"

I picked up my remaining half a doughnut and stuffed it into my mouth with both hands. (Since I'm not allowed to talk with my mouth full, I knew I wouldn't have to confess—not right away, anyway. Also, guilty or not, there's no good reason to waste a doughnut.)

"Doing what?" Grandma Bernice said, all innocent-like.

Mama slipped out of her clacky shoes and dropped them into the shoe basket. "You know what," she said, giving Grandma a stern look.

Grandma crossed her arms over her chest and managed to look insulted.

Mama grabbed the newspaper and held it up as evidence of our crimes. "It's not natural, not *normal*, to talk so much about death. It's unhealthy."

"It's not unhealthy. Death's part of life," Grandma said, getting up from the table.

"Maybe for you and your friends," Mama said, shaking the newspaper at Grandma, "but I keep tellin' you, Lula Bell is only a child! She doesn't need to worry about *death* right now!"

"Hmph!" Grandma Bernice said on her way out of the kitchen.

I wanted to shout, *I am not a child! I am ten!* But the angry way Mama wadded up the newspaper and tossed it into the trash stopped me. Instead, I said as casually as I could, "Hey, Mama, I've been meanin' to ask you: could you teach me to make curls in my hair using bobby pins, like Grandma Bernice does?"

"Pin curls won't work on you," Mama said. "Grandma Bernice's hair is different than yours. She has some natural curl."

This was very disappointing news.

Mama came over and kissed the top of my head. "You have beautiful hair."

"No, I don't. I have boring hair," I said, and it was true. My hair was stick-straight and boring brown.

"Good night!" Grandma Bernice hollered from upstairs.

"Good night!" Mama and I hollered back in unison.

"Did you and Alan finish your science project?" Mama asked as she carried my glass and plate to the kitchen sink.

"Yes, ma'am," I said. "Our tornado box is all ready for the science fair on Monday night."

Mama looked impressed. "Exactly how do you make a tornado?"

"It's pretty simple. All you need is a corner, a fan, and a humidifier."

"What if your fan or your humidifier fails? Do you have a backup?" Mama asked.

"A backup?" I repeated. "A backup fan and a backup humidifier? Um, no, ma'am."

"Hmmm . . . well, maybe you ought to think about that."

"Yes, ma'am," I said, knowing I would do no such thing. I mean, the thought of lugging one fan and one humidifier to school was bad enough. The thought of hauling in a backup fan and a backup humidifier was even worse. I figured I might as well write "I am a total geek" across my forehead and wear a backup T-shirt that said the same thing, in case my forehead message failed.

The grandfather clock on the stairs rang out in song and then gonged the hour for all to hear. Just the reminder Mama needed to say, "Go get ready for bed now."

Poopoopahduke! I thought as I got up from the table and pushed my chair in.

Mama turned the faucet on and started rinsing dishes.

On my way out of the kitchen, I paused and said, "You know, Grandma Bernice's birthday is next week, and I think she might like a party. Daddy'll be home over the weekend, too."

Mama turned the faucet off, rolled her eyes, and

nodded, as if to say, *Well, of course Grandma Bernice would like a party.* But what she actually said was, "Couldn't we talk about this tomorrow?"

"Because you're still mad at Grandma Bernice? About . . . our . . . um, *activities?*" (Over the years, Grandma's preoccupation with death had become a real sore spot with Mama.)

"No, Lula Bell," Mama huffed. "I'm just tired is all."

She was still mad—I could tell—but Mama never admits to being mad. "Mad" is rude; "tired" is more polite, apparently.

"It's my fault, Mama," I tried. "I wanted Grandma to wait up for me because I wanted—"

Mama let out a breathy little laugh. "Honey, Grandma Bernice would've waited up, with dough-nuts, for both of us, no matter what. She's been wait-ing up with doughnuts for me for more than thirty years now! Why, growing up, I ate doughnuts after every school play and church Christmas pageant, after every ballet recital, after final exams—where do you think I got these hips?"

"You must've done a really good job," I said. "You must've done *a lot* of really good jobs."

The way Mama looked at me then . . . well, I don't think she took that as a compliment.

"So . . . then . . . um, maybe if I'm a big star in the talent show at school, there might be doughnuts afterward?" I blurted, desperate to distract Mama from her hips. True, I didn't especially want to talk about the talent show, but it was better than talking about hips. *Anything* was better than talking about hips. (Here's a little tip for you: hips—and butts—are not safe topics with mamas.)

"Lula Bell, your daddy and I have discussed this. You *will* be in the talent show," Mama said seriously. Then, her face softened as she said, "And I'm sure there will be doughnuts afterward."

My stomach did a somersault. It was one thing to fantasize about being the star of the talent show—which I did all the time, picturing kids hoisting me up on their shoulders and carrying me through the school, like the star basketball player who sank the winning shot in the last second of the championship game—but reality was something else.

In the real world, I knew that it was always a mistake to call attention to myself at school. Always. And really, is there a bigger, bolder way to call attention to yourself than declaring, "Hey, y'all! I have talent! Watch this!" Because that's what being in a talent show pretty much amounts to—don't you think? Yeah, I'm pretty sure that bringing *talent* to school is way worse than bringing *tuna*.

A Moody Morning

When I came downstairs on Friday morning, Mama was sitting at the kitchen table, making the grocery list.

"Good mornin', Lula Bell," she said, glancing up from her list.

"Mornin'," I said, taking my seat at the kitchen table.

Grandma Bernice smiled at me as she pulled her black iron skillet off the stove.

I smiled back and then said to Mama, "Um, could you add Choc-O-Crunch cereal to that list?"

Mama stopped writing and looked up. "No,

Lula Bell. No more cereal. You never eat it—after you get the prize out, it just sits on the shelf going stale until I throw it away."

"Please, Mama. There's a collectable Detective Delicious magnifying glass in every box of Choc-O-Crunch—while supplies last—and I'll eat the cereal this time, I promise."

"No," Mama said quietly, and then she went back to her list.

Grandma slid a plate of bacon, eggs, and biscuits in front of me and untied her apron, revealing a baby-blue sweat suit that was still creased from ironing. (Grandma Bernice always wore sweat suits, which I don't really understand, because I never once saw her exercise—or sweat.)

"Thank you," I mumbled. I was still thinking about that magnifying glass and feeling disappointed. The way I saw it, that magnifying glass was about all I needed to become Nancy Drew—in the privacy of my own home, of course.

Grandma gave my shoulder a sympathetic squeeze and then sat down just as Mama stood up. She tightened the belt on the red-and-white kimono that Daddy had bought her when his band was touring China last year. (Daddy plays the steel guitar in a country band called Boots and Whistles, so he's gone—on tour with his band—most of the time.) Then, she carried her coffee cup to the kitchen sink and rinsed it before starting in on supper.

It was always like this. Grandma Bernice was in charge of breakfast, but the minute she sat down in the mornings, Mama got up, because she was in charge of supper, and Mama liked to get a jump on supper, even if it was 6:30 a.m. (Grandma said that's because Mama believes in the three *p*'s: be prepared, be punctual, and be practical.)

As I buttered my biscuit, Grandma Bernice announced, "I'd like lobster soup for supper tonight. I've been craving lobster soup all week. I even dreamed of lobster soup last night!"

Mama shook her head absently as she sliced a purple onion. "I've already got the chicken thawing." That meant no. Once my mama had meat thawing, that was it; there was no changing meal plans.

"So?" Grandma Bernice said. "Go wild! Put the chicken back in the refrig! What'll it hurt? I really want lobster soup."

Mama stopped slicing, looked up, and said firmly, "It's lobster *bisque*, and the answer's no."

41

Grandma Bernice sighed and shook her head. "Okay, but you'll be sorry one day. I am *not* a young woman."

Mama shot Grandma Bernice a look that said, *It's too early in the morning to start planning your death again.*

But Grandma pretended not to notice and stared out the window. "Look! Look!" she said suddenly, pointing.

Mama and I looked. There was a red cardinal perched on our hummingbird feeder, admiring his own reflection in our window. At least, that's what I thought, until he flew into the glass with such tremendous force, I was sure he'd knocked himself out cold.

I looked at Grandma with wide eyes.

"He thought he saw another bird movin' in on his territory," Grandma explained.

"Do you think he's okay?" I asked.

"Oh yes," Grandma said, waving a hand through the air. "He'll be fine."

Sure enough, that cardinal popped right back up on the hummingbird feeder.

"I'll need to put food in that feeder soon," Grandma said. "My hummingbirds'll be back in no time. I hope I see the white one again."

"Mother, I *told* you," Mama said, "you did not see any white hummingbird. Hummingbirds aren't white."

"And *I* told *you* I *did* see a white hummingbird, right here in our very own backyard!" Grandma said to Mama.

They stared each other down. If looks were wind, Mama's would've knocked Grandma Bernice over backward in her chair. If looks were lightning, the one Grandma shot back at Mama would've instantly set her on fire. None of that happened, of course, but neither of them gave up trying.

I kept my eyes on my breakfast, concentrating hard on chewing a slice of bacon. For a few minutes, it was so quiet that all we could hear was my chomping—even with my mouth closed.

Then, Grandma Bernice turned to me and asked, "Lula Bell, do you believe in reincarnation?"

"What's that?" I said with a mouth full of biscuit.

"Don't talk with your mouth full; it's rude," Mama warned.

"It's when you die and you come back to life as something else," Grandma Bernice said, her eyes glowing with excitement.

"Something else?"

Grandma nodded. "Like an animal or an insect or something."

"An insect?" I made a face.

"Like a butterfly!" Grandma said, flapping her hands like wings.

I considered this and then said, "But butterflies only live about two weeks."

"That's okay," Grandma said easily, "because I'm not going to come back as a butterfly. I'm going to come back as a hummingbird—a *solid white* hummingbird! Do you think that's possible, Lula Bell?"

I opened my mouth to say something, but before I could, Mama slammed her knife down on the cutting board.

Grandma and I both jumped, and I thought to myself, *Boy, is Mama tired* (translation: mad) *this morning!*

"Enough!" Mama said. "No more talk about death. Mother, can't you see you're scaring Lula Bell?"

(It was Mama who was scaring me, not Grandma Bernice.)

"Hmph!" Grandma Bernice said.

"Um, I gotta go," I said. "I don't want to miss my bus."

Oddly enough, that was the truth. Usually, I

dreaded the bus—and the bus stop—something awful. But on that particular morning, I figured anyplace would be better than my kitchen—especially if there was no chance of me getting that magnifying glass, which there wasn't now that everybody was in such a bad mood.

Bullies and Grizzlies and Wolves—Oh My!

I'd forgotten that Alan wouldn't be at the bus stop that morning, that his dad had volunteered to transport our tornado box—humidifier and all (thank you! thank you!)—to school, until I got down to the bus stop. Who did I find there? Kali Keele.

I gave her lots of personal space and avoided direct eye contact. In other words, I treated Kali the way you'd treat a grizzly bear, and for the same reason: so as not to challenge her in any way.

Kali gave me a hard look, up and down, up and down. But then, finally, she looked away without saying anything.

I didn't say anything either, but how could I not be aware of this admittedly small but no less vicious grizzly bear with perfectly styled blond hair moving around me?

When the bus arrived, I let Kali go on ahead of me while I knelt in the grass and pretended to fool with something in my backpack. But as soon as I climbed onto the bus, Kali started whispering to her friends. They all looked me up and down, just like Kali had.

I planted my behind as soon as I could, on the very first seat, right behind the bus driver—where no one ever sits, not even the first graders. (Here's a little tip for you: the seat right behind the bus driver is the uncoolest seat on the bus. If your teacher rode the bus to school with you, that's where she'd sit. It's where she sits on field trips, isn't it? However, given a choice between being uncool and being attacked by Kali, I recommend uncool.)

I got lucky on the bus that morning. But I knew from experience that my luck wouldn't hold. Apparently, I wasn't the only one who knew it.

At lunchtime, Alan—and his hair—tailed me through the noisy cafeteria, through the lunch line, and finally to a table, where he sat down across from me, like he did almost every day. (Except for whenever I got up my courage and tried sitting at the girls' table. Then Alan sat with Richard and Bill. They seemed to have a sort of second-choice understanding. Richard and Bill chose each other first, and Alan chose me.)

"I apologize, Lula Bell," Alan said as soon as he sat down. "I should've offered you a ride to school this morning."

"Oh no, that's okay," I said, and it really was, because the only thing uncooler than riding to school right behind the bus driver would've been riding to school with Alan West.

Alan unfolded his napkin and placed it in his lap. "So . . . then . . . everything went all right this morning?"

"Sure," I said, like I had no idea what Alan was talking about or why he might've been worried.

Alan nodded as he speared one of his chicken nuggets with his fork. "Good."

I busied myself with opening my milk.

"Did you happen to catch the program about wolves on the Animal Channel last night?" Alan asked.

I felt myself relax a little. "No. Was it good?"

"Fascinating," Alan said. "Wolves actually prefer psychological—or emotional—warfare over physical fighting. Their status within the pack is mostly based on how they act, not on how they fight."

I nodded as I picked up a chicken nugget.

"The most powerful wolves, the alphas and betas, are the ones that act the most confident, but they aren't necessarily the biggest or the strongest. The weakest wolves, the omegas, act submissive, or passive—they always back down, never stand their ground, not even when they could easily win."

I stared at Alan.

"The omegas are the wolves that all the other wolves pick on," he added.

I looked around to make sure no one else was listening, then leaned over the table and said, "What are you trying to say?" My voice sounded strangled and hurt, which only made me feel more pathetic.

"Nothing," Alan said calmly. "I know how you like the Animal Channel, that's all."

It was a lie, and we both knew it. I did like the Animal Channel—I loved it, as a matter of fact, but that wasn't why Alan was telling me about the wolves. Even so, I was glad—grateful even—that

Alan had lied to me. I mean, it's one thing to know that you're the weakling, the omega wolf—privately. It's another thing to be called the omega wolf, out loud, by someone who isn't even trying to hurt you but who wants to help you. Because there's really no denying it then, is there?

Playing Possurtle

That afternoon, I chose my seat on the bus carefully—not too near the front and not too near the back, but somewhere in the middle, where I at least had a chance at going unnoticed. I sat there alone, squinching down in my seat, keeping to myself. I didn't talk to anyone, didn't look at anyone, didn't so much as turn my head to look out the window—I even *breathed* quietly.

Grandma Bernice would've said I was "playing possum," since possums pretend to be dead when threatened, and she would've been right. Sort of. Except that I was also playing turtle. I made myself as small as possible, clung to my backpack like it was a shield, and sort of balled myself up around it so that I couldn't be seen over the top or around the sides of my seat. Honestly, I would've climbed *into* my backpack if I could've, like a turtle hiding in its shell. So it'd probably be more accurate to say I was playing possurtle. And just in case that wasn't enough, I thought to myself, *I'm not here. I'm not here. You don't see me, because I'm not here.*

And it worked. Almost. Until Kali called out from the back of the bus, "Hey, Lula Bell, I know what you're doing—*everybody* knows what you're doing—and it won't work."

I had no idea what she was talking about. I wasn't *doing* anything. On purpose.

Everyone got quiet, like maybe they were playing possum—or possurtle—too.

Kali continued, "Everybody knows that I wore a blue Sassy-Brand shirt with jeans yesterday, and everybody knows *you're* wearing a blue shirt with jeans today because you're tryin' to be just like me."

I wasn't trying to be just like Kali; I was trying to avoid being picked on. I'd figured nobody would make fun of clothes similar to their own, because then they'd sort of be making fun of themselves, right? But I hadn't thought of the copycat angle.

Naturally, Kali hollered, "You're nothin' but a big old copycat, Lula Bell Bonner, and everybody knows it, so you can just stop it! Do you hear me? Just *stop it*!"

I felt my face get hot, but I just sat there, staring at the white crack in the leather-like fabric on the back of the seat in front of me. My fingers wanted to pick at the rip, to peel the leather back from the white fabric underneath, but I didn't move. I was as still as a stone, except for my toes, which were wiggling like crazy. I knew my stop couldn't be more than thirty seconds away, so I started counting in my mind: *one-Mississippi, two-Mississippi* . . .

"I'm going to burn my blue shirt as soon as I get home," I heard Kali announce to her friends.

Out of the corner of my eye, I could see Alan West—and his life-of-its-own hair—watching me from across the aisle. Alan moved his hand back and forth, trying to get my attention.

But I ignored him and kept right on counting: . . . *ten-Mississippi, eleven-Mississippi* . . . until the bus screeched to a stop. Then I launched myself out of there like a rocket.

"Lula Bell!" I heard Alan call after me as I hurried toward my house. "Lula Bell! Wait up!"

But I didn't. I didn't stop, didn't wait, didn't slow down, didn't even turn around. Just didn't.

A Party!

By the time we pulled into our driveway after church on Sunday, I was so excited, I could hardly stand it. It was the day of Grandma Bernice's birthday party—a surprise! Plus, Daddy had pulled in late last night from Alabama, and I hadn't gotten to see him yet. *C'mon! C'mon!* I thought. Nobody had been moving fast enough for me that morning, especially not Pastor Dan, who'd just gone on and on, waaay past the time that church was supposed to let out. (If you are a preacher, here's a little tip for you: stick to the schedule.)

"I think I'll have a 'mater sandwich for lunch," Grandma Bernice said, heaving her car door open.

(A 'mater sandwich is really a BLT—a bacon, lettuce, and tomato sandwich—but Grandma Bernice considered the tomato—the 'mater—the important part. The other stuff amounted to toppings.)

I was the first one out of the car. Mama got out next. Finally, Grandma's white head popped up. But then she started moving in the wrong direction, away from our house. Mama and I walked around the car, just as Grandma Bernice bent to pick up a soda can in our next door neighbor's driveway.

"The dogs got loose again," Grandma said, straightening. She held her back with one hand and the soda can with the other hand, while her little purse swung back and forth from her wrist. Behind Grandma Bernice, the Lanhams' trash can lay toppled on its side, torn-up trash bags and yuck scattered all around it.

Mama and I exchanged a look.

"Well?" Grandma said, squinting against the noon sun.

"Go and help her, Lula Bell," Mama said.

"But that's not even *our* trash," I complained in a voice barely above a whisper. (I didn't want Grandma Bernice to hear. I knew she'd say that we were always supposed to leave a place nicer than we found it, but I figured whoever made up that rule probably meant to add "unless you're on your way to a party.")

Mama turned and gave me a look that read, *Keep on complaining and you'll find yourself taking care of trash for everyone on Cherry Tree Lane.*

"Lula Bell! You know you should always leave a place nicer than you found it," Grandma said, sounding shocked and disappointed all at once. (See? I told you.)

When Grandma Bernice, Mama, and I finished picking up the Lanhams' garbage and went inside—finally!—everybody in our living room yelled, "SURPRISE!"

Flash! Flash! Flash! went Daddy's camera.

I smiled at him.

Daddy lowered the camera and smiled back.

He needed a haircut, I noticed, but then Daddy almost always needs a haircut.

When I looked over at Grandma Bernice, her mouth was hanging open, and she had a hand over her heart. Her eyes wandered over each of the faces—friends from her quilting bee, her Sunday school class, our neighborhood, and Mama's beauty shop. When she spotted her brother, Cleburne, who'd come all the way from Louisville, Kentucky, Grandma's eyes got watery.

"Clee," Grandma Bernice said softly, taking a step toward him, "I thought I'd never see you again."

Great Uncle Cleburne smiled and held on to his walker for dear life as Grandma threw her arms around him and hugged with all her might. "Happy birthday, Bernice," he said.

Grandma pulled back and took a good, long look at her brother. "Oh Clee, honey, where did your beautiful hair go?" she said sadly.

"What do you mean!" Great Uncle Cleburne said, reaching up to feel of the top of his head with one hand. He looked shocked and mighty upset to find skin there—just skin.

Grandma's eyes bulged and her cheeks turned pink. "Oh . . . well now . . . I . . . I didn't mean . . .," she stammered, looking around the room for help.

No one said a word.

Slowly, a smile spread across Great Uncle Cleburne's face. "I'm just joshin' you," he said. "I knew it was gone, darlin'."

I was so relieved, I laughed out loud.

"Bernice, you remember my oldest daughter,

Ethel," Great Uncle Cleburne said, tilting his head toward the lady next to him. "She lives in Texas." (Ethel looked a lot like Mama, I thought, only she was bigger and her hair wasn't as pretty.)

Grandma hugged Ethel, too.

Once we'd washed up, we had not only 'mater sandwiches but lobster soup and pecan pie—all Grandma Bernice's favorites—for lunch. All afternoon and into the evening, the house was crowded with noise and happiness. Great Uncle Cleburne and his daughter, Ethel, who I figured was probably some sort of cousin to me, stayed the longest.

After second helpings of sandwiches, soup, and pie, we cleaned up. Mama transferred food, wrapped it up, and put it away. Cousin Ethel washed dishes, and I dried.

"Uncle Cleburne is such a character," Mama said, smiling, as she handed Cousin Ethel a china platter.

"You have no idea," Cousin Ethel said seriously. "Why, just yesterday morning, I was in the car, listening to a talk show on the radio, when I heard the host say, 'Let's take some calls. First, we'll hear from Cleburne in Louisville, Kentucky.'"

"*No*," Mama said with wide eyes.

Ethel nodded. "And there he was on the radio, ranting and raving for the entire country to hear!"

Mama laughed. We all did.

"Oh, c'mon, Bernice, pleeease," Great Uncle Cleburne was begging when I came back downstairs from changing into my pajamas.

Grandma pretended to feel highly put upon, but I could tell that she was secretly pleased. "Oh, for heaven's sake, all right!" she said as she pushed herself up from her lazy-girl chair.

Grandma waited for me to squeeze in on the couch between Mama and Daddy. Then she sat down at our old upright piano and began playing and singing the hymn "Amazing Grace." Great Uncle Cleburne joined Grandma Bernice, singing harmony. It truly was amazing.

Then Grandma called out, "Your turn, Lula Bell!"

"No, thank you," I said, smiling sweetly at Great Uncle Cleburne and Cousin Ethel.

Grandma turned to look at me over her shoulder.

I gave her a look back that read, *No. Forget it. I am not kidding around here!*

"Oh! I know! How 'bout the song you've been

working on for the talent show at school?" Grandma said hopefully.

I shook my head.

Grandma faced the piano and played a few bars of "This Little Light of Mine," holding the last note and turning to ask me again with her eyes.

My bare toes waggled around in the carpet as I shook my head again.

Grandma finally took the pressure off me by playing another song. This time, Great Uncle Cleburne joined in on "I'll Fly Away."

I felt grateful but guilty, relieved but disappointed in myself. This resulted in a lot of nervous, overzealous clapping on my part.

"Thank you," Grandma Bernice said as she got up from the piano.

I kept right on clapping.

Everyone started giving me strange, confused, uncomfortable kinds of looks—except for Uncle Cleburne. I decided I liked him a lot.

"Thank you," Grandma said again, looking directly at me, as if to say, *Enough.*

Daddy placed a large hand over both my hands and gently lowered them to my lap.

I looked at him and with my eyes, I tried to say,

Thanks! I don't know what came over me!

Daddy grinned.

"No, thank *you*," Great Uncle Cleburne was saying. "If you only knew how I'd longed to hear you sing again, Bernice."

Grandma glowed with pride. "You should hear Lula Bell."

"You should hear Daddy," I said.

Daddy's grin widened, showing his dimple. "Another time," he said. Then he put his arm around me, squeezed, and whispered into my ear, "Thanks, sweetie, but this is Grandma Bernice's night."

"Thank you, all of you, for the best birthday I ever had," Grandma said.

"And it's not even your birthday yet!" I said, because Grandma Bernice's actual birthday wasn't until the next day.

Grandma winked and nodded at me as she sat back down in her lazy-girl chair.

As the grown-ups talked and reminisced, my eyes grew heavy, but I stayed put. I was determined not to miss a thing. The last thing I heard that night before I fell asleep on the couch was Grandma Bernice saying, "Remember when you went to work on the Purnell's pig farm, Clee?"

Great Uncle Cleburne chuckled. Then, all the warm, comfortable, happy feelings in the room closed around me like an old quilt and carried me off to sleep.

A Bumpy Beginning

I was still on the couch, nestled under one of Grandma Bernice's oldest and softest quilts, when Mama woke me up on Monday morning.

"We overslept! We're late! You've gotta hurry, Lula Bell!" Mama said.

I just blinked at her and tried to make sense of the words gushing from her lips, like Honey Run Creek after a good storm.

Mama stood and tossed clothes on top of the quilt, on top of me. "Put these on. Hurry! And then I'll drive you to school."

My brain was sleepy and slow to add up our

problem. Whatever it was, I knew it couldn't be *that* serious, seeing as how Mama still had bed-head and was wearing her kimono—if disaster was on the way, Mama surely would've brushed her hair and dressed to meet it. Even so, I shook sleep off and did as I was told.

"Now run upstairs and brush your teeth—quietly," Mama said.

"Can't I say good-bye to Daddy and Grandma Bernice?"

"No, Lula Bell, let them sleep—they were up awfully late."

"But I *always* say good-bye to Grandma Bernice, and Daddy'll be gone when I get back from school," I pleaded.

Mama was losing her patience. "We don't have time. Now go brush your teeth and come straight back."

I pouted a little but followed her instructions.

Mama was waiting by the garage door, car keys in hand, monster-purse hanging from her shoulder, when I came back downstairs. Although she'd brushed her hair, she still looked a little funny wearing her purse with her red and white kimono and neon blue fuzzy slippers, but I shouldn't have been surprised; my mama will do just about anything to stay on schedule. (Let her be an example to you, Pastor Dan.)

I dug my shoes out of the shoe basket and put them on my feet, then checked the clock over the stove. "I hope you wrote me a note."

"What?" Mama said.

I grabbed my backpack. "I'm late. So you can either come into the school and sign me in or send a note—I hope you wrote a note."

"Oh. Just a second. I'll write the note."

"I sure hope you don't get pulled over by the police or anything," I said once Mama and I were in the car—because one time, we saw a lady in Nashville being handcuffed by the police *in her pajamas!*

"Me, too," Mama said, smiling for the first time that morning as she stepped on the gas with her furry blue foot.

I never really settled into a rhythm at school that day. The running-late-ness stayed with me through language arts, math, lunch, and social studies. Even though I frantically tried to catch up, I was always a step behind everybody else: the last one to find the right page in my textbook, the last one to find a pencil, the last one through the lunch line, and then I couldn't find my social studies homework, so I had to dig through my backpack, book by book, page by page, to come up with it while my whole class waited. It felt as if the world had shifted while I slept, and I couldn't regain my balance. Little did I know the world hadn't shifted. It had ended.

The End of My World

Since I'd missed the bus that morning—and therefore Kali had missed her chance to torment me—I went into possurtle position as soon as I got on the bus that afternoon. Now, I know what you're thinking, but sometimes it works. Sometimes. But not that day. (That's probably because Alan West sat down beside me, and his hair doesn't do possurtle. It's too busy standing up and saying things like *Ta-dah!*)

Anyway, that day Kali Keele called out from the back of the bus, "Hey, Lula Bell!" She seemed to be waiting for me to turn around. Which I didn't.

"Hey!" Kali shouted louder. "Lula Bell, I'm talkin' to you!"

I pretended not to hear her—again.

Alan turned and looked at me.

I stared straight ahead but wanted to yell at him, *No! Don't look at me! Pretend I'm not here!* But I didn't say a thing—to Alan or Kali.

Even so, Kali kept it up. It was as if I'd turned around and said, "What?" Because the next thing she said was, "I saw you and your grandma picking up trash yesterday—are y'all like the neighborhood janitors now?"

I heard a few snickers. There were two more stops before mine. I thought about getting off at both of them and walking the rest of the way home. But what if the driver noticed me getting off at the wrong stop, got after me in front of everybody, and made me sit back down? No point in embarrassing myself—even more—especially if I couldn't actually get off the bus. So, I just sat there, waiting and wiggling my toes so hard I'm surprised my shoes didn't go flying off.

The bus hadn't even come to a complete stop when I sprang out of my seat and started pushing past Alan—almost ending up in his lap. I thought

Alan looked a little surprised, but with that hair, who knows?

As I hovered over him, hanging on to the seat in front of us, Alan whispered, "The biggest mistake one can make with a wolf is to run. *Don't* run."

Of course, as soon as I regained my balance, I threw myself down the aisle, cleared the steps in one mighty leap, and took off running without looking back.

I slammed the front door behind me and leaned against it, trying to catch my breath.

"Lula Bell," Daddy said in a hoarse voice.

When my eyes had adjusted to the darkness, I found Daddy sitting on the couch. He patted the seat beside him.

Something was wrong. Daddy wasn't supposed to be here, and the house was way too dark. Dread filled me and I hesitated, not wanting to know whatever it was. But just like that morning, I told myself it couldn't be *that* bad, and that everything was okay—or soon would be. I lowered my backpack to the floor, meandered over to the couch, and plunked myself down.

Daddy's eyes were red and swollen. Had he been

crying? Is that why all the curtains were closed—
because Daddy didn't want anybody to see him
crying? I was pretty sure Daddy didn't cry. Ever.
Must be allergies, I decided.

Daddy took my hand in his and cleared his
throat with some effort.

Yep, allergies, I thought.

"Lula Bell," Daddy said, "Grandma Bernice is . . .
gone."

I nodded. "Where'd she go?"

"To heaven, honey."

"Huh?" I said, because I hadn't been thinking
in terms of heaven; I'd been thinking in terms of
Al's Food Valu or Jo-Ann's Fabrics.

"Grandma Bernice has gone to heaven," Daddy
said.

I shook my head, as if to say, *No, no, no, no.*

Daddy nodded his, just barely, as if to whisper,
Yes, yes, yes, yes.

"That's not true!" I said, my voice rising in
panic. "It couldn't be! I just saw Grandma Bernice
last night! She was fine! She was *singing!*"

"I know," Daddy said quietly.

His words didn't make sense. "Are you saying
that Grandma Bernice *died*?"

Daddy lowered his eyes so that I couldn't see them and nodded again.

"How did she die?" I demanded to know.

"In her sleep, early this morning. I'm so sorry, Lula Bell."

I shot up off the couch and ran for the stairs.

Upstairs, I hesitated in front of Grandma Bernice's closed bedroom door, afraid of what I might find on the other side. My heart pounded against my chest. I kept sucking in air, but it never seemed to reach my lungs. I took a deep breath, forced it all the way down, held it, and opened the door.

Grandma's room was too still, too quiet, and too clean. Her bed had been made in a way that somehow told me she hadn't made it herself. There was no clutter: no hairbrush lying next to a pile of bobby pins on the dresser, no bootie-slippers on the floor next to the bed, no fabric remnants anywhere. And there was not a speck of dust.

That's when I knew that Daddy had been telling the truth. The air left my lungs in a whoosh, like a balloon deflating. I took one step forward and crumpled onto Grandma's bed.

Horrible, sad sounds filled Grandma Bernice's

room—the kind of sounds mother seals make while their babies are being clubbed to death on the ice, right in front of them. I clamped my hands over my ears.

That's when I realized the sounds were coming from *me.*

Life Goes On—How Rude!

The next few mornings were the hardest. I'd forget while I was sleeping. Then, when I woke up, I'd remember. And remembering was like hearing the news for the first time, all over again. At first, I'd think—hope—that maybe it was all just a bad dream. When I realized it wasn't, I'd close my eyes and pray. I'd tell God that I would do anything, *anything*, if He would just let Grandma Bernice be okay, if He would just give her back. But He didn't.

On Thursday morning, when I finally opened my eyes, the first thing I saw was a black dress, which appeared to be my size, hanging on the back of Grandma Bernice's bedroom door; it still had tags dangling from the underarm. Below that, on the floor, were shiny, black patent-leather shoes with straps that buckled on the sides. A pair of lacy white socks stuck out from inside one of the shoes. The other shoe held clean underwear. These things were to be my funeral clothes, I knew. I guessed Mama had left them here because I hadn't slept in my own room in days, and because Grandma Bernice's funeral was today. I didn't know how to feel about that, but I did know that I had to be there no matter what.

When I went downstairs, I found Mama bustling around the kitchen. She, too, had on a black dress—with her blue fuzzy slippers.

Mama looked up. "You look nice, Lula Bell."

"Thanks," I mumbled.

"Would you get the cake knife out of that drawer," Mama asked, pointing, "and put it on the table, please?"

I nodded, looking around. Our kitchen table held two chocolate-frosted cakes, one white-frosted cake, banana pudding, a pecan pie, a stack of dessert plates, a stack of napkins, and now, a cake knife. Had Mama been up baking all night? That seemed . . . wrong. It *all* seemed wrong.

"Ummm . . . what are you doing?" I asked, because Mama couldn't have been doing what I thought she was doing.

Mama set a heavy stack of plates out on the counter. "Preparing," was all she said.

I decided not to press her further, because after all, Mama was Grandma Bernice's daughter. But when I walked into our living room and saw three card tables set up and draped with white table-cloths, just like the ones we'd had at Grandma Bernice's birthday party four days earlier, I changed my mind.

I poked my head back into the kitchen and said, "Ummm . . . we're not having a *party*, are we?" I mean, what kind of party could we possibly have been having today? Surely we weren't having a 'Hooray! Grandma Bernice Is Dead!' party.

"No," Mama said, "it's not exactly a party."

I waited for more of an explanation.

Mama set a tray of silverware on the counter and placed a stack of napkins next to it. Then, she stepped back and inspected her work from left to right: napkins, silverware, plates, a long stretch of counter, and at the end, four rows of upside-down water glasses next to a big ice bucket.

I sighed—mostly just to remind Mama that I was there, waiting.

Mama gave a small nod of approval and then looked at me. "I don't really know what you call it," she finally said, "but after a funeral, people go to the family's house and remember and . . . just sort of keep one another company."

It looked like a party to me, but I didn't say so. Neither of us said anything else until a car honked outside.

"Oh!" Mama checked her watch. "The car's here—it's time to go."

I thought to myself, *Well, of course our car's here. Where else would it be? But who's honking our horn, and isn't that rude?*

Mama hollered for Daddy, grabbed her purse, and started for the front door—then she remembered to change out of her slippers and into her dress-up shoes. Too bad Daddy didn't think to change *his* shoes.

For the first time that I knew of, Daddy wore a suit and tie. For the first time, he looked like all the other daddies. Until you noticed his feet. (Here's a little tip for you: your old, beat-up brown cowboy boots might not go perfectly with your slick new black suit. I'm just saying: consider all your options.)

When I stepped out onto the front porch, I couldn't believe my eyes: what was that long, glossy black limousine doing parked in our driveway? I turned to look at Mama.

She lowered her head and seemed embarrassed. "I know, I know. It's *so* ostentatious," she said, "but Grandma Bernice arranged for us to ride in this limo, and she'd already paid for it—all nonrefundable."

"I think it's nice," Daddy said, smiling a sad little smile.

"Nonrefundable?" I whispered to Daddy as we hurried toward the limo.

Daddy nodded. "Yeah, your mama couldn't get Grandma Bernice's money back, but she tried."

I think I would've enjoyed riding in a limo on any other day. It was spacious and plush. But as it was, I just stared out the window. The sky was dark and threatened rain, which suited me just fine. It would've seemed wrong for the sun to shine today.

It did seem wrong for the rest of the world to go right on, like nothing much had happened. People had put out their trash like it was an ordinary day, and the garbage truck in front of us stopped to collect it like it was an ordinary day. Impatient drivers whizzed past us. A mother scolded her son in the parking lot of the Mapco station. The man in the car behind us talked on his phone.

I wanted to roll down the window and holler, *Hey! Stop what you're doing! Something horrible has happened! Grandma Bernice has left the world!* But when I looked down at all the silver buttons on the limo door, I knew I'd never find the one that worked the window in time to speak to any of these people. And anyway, they didn't know Grandma Bernice. I felt sort of sorry for them then. They'd missed their chance.

I turned away from the window feeling somehow lucky. Lucky because I hadn't missed my chance. I'd known Grandma Bernice my whole life. In fact, the only way I could've had more time with her was if I'd been born sooner. And the fact that I hadn't been born sooner—well, that certainly wasn't my fault.

Daddy reached over then and covered my hand with his. His hand felt warm and big and strong.

I tried to smile at him.

He smiled back.

Mama reached across Daddy and put her hand on top of Daddy's, on top of mine. We all exchanged looks. Our looks seemed to say, *We're all in this together. We're going to be okay. Probably.*

The Funeral

AS soon as we opened the door to the church, I could smell them. And when we entered the sanctuary, the sight took my breath away. We stood frozen in place, staring at what must've been every flower in the state of Tennessee, gathered together in one room. I'd never seen so many flowers, so many kinds, so many colors. I didn't even know that many flowers existed.

"Grandma Bernice would've loved this," Mama said to no one in particular.

"She really would have," Daddy agreed.

When I came to my senses, I said, "But where are all the people?"

Grandma Bernice had hoped to "really pack 'em in" at her funeral. I knew, because she'd told me.

"We're having a few minutes of private visitation, just for family, first," Mama said.

I learned that "private visitation" meant we were all supposed to visit Grandma Bernice, who was parked down front in the sanctuary, in her casket, to say good-bye.

We took turns. I went last, and Mama came with me. Only, when I got up there, I couldn't say good-bye, because I couldn't speak. As soon as I saw Grandma Bernice, my throat tightened, and I began coughing and crying all at once.

Mama must've thought that I was choking because she slapped me—hard—on the back.

I looked up at Mama, stunned.

"You all right?" Mama said.

"Her mouth," I croaked, "there's something wrong with her mouth—that doesn't look like Grandma Bernice at all!"

Mama's face relaxed, and she put her arms around me. "It isn't Grandma Bernice, honey," she whispered into my hair. "Bodies are like houses, and that's just an old house Grandma Bernice used to live in."

After that, there was a brief visitation for everybody else who wanted to say good-bye to Grandma Bernice. People kept saying things like, "She looks so pretty" or "so peaceful" or "so natural." I wanted to shout, *She does not! Did you even know my Grandma Bernice?* But I didn't. Instead, I sat quietly in the front pew, just like Mama had told me to.

My piano and voice teacher, Mrs. West, arrived with Alan while people were still milling around. Mrs. West went right to Mama. Alan came right to me.

"You look pretty," he tried.

"I do not," I snapped, as if he had insulted me.

But Alan just bowed his head and said quietly, "You do. You're the prettiest girl I ever saw, Lula Bell."

I crossed my arms over my chest and glared up at him. I mean, my eyes were swollen and red; my nose was swollen and red—basically, from the neck up, I was swollen, red, and splotchy. I was not having a good day. Did Alan think he could make it better by lying to me? Or worse, was he *teasing* me about the way I looked?

But then Alan's eyes met mine, and there was

something in them that told me he meant what he'd said. I uncrossed my arms and tried to think what I should say. I had no idea, so I just said what I was thinking: "Um . . . were you at school the day they tested our vision?"

Alan gave me a half smile.

"How many fingers am I holding up?" I asked him.

"Three."

He was right. *Huh.*

Mama and Daddy came over then, thanked Alan for coming, and seated themselves on either side of me.

When Great Uncle Cleburne and Cousin Ethel arrived and took the last two seats beside us, the funeral began. It was as if Grandma had instructed, "Don't start until every seat is filled—wait 'til Sunday morning if you have to!" She might've even said those exact words; it wouldn't have surprised me.

Just as Grandma Bernice had decided how and when she wanted to go—every week—she'd decided every detail of her send-off. She'd planned every detail of her funeral in advance. I'm pretty sure she even told Pastor Dan what to say.

Pastor Dan delivered the eulogy, which is kind of like a sermon, and the main message was this: Bernice Bell wants you to get out there. Live! Laugh! Love! And above all, let your light shine! The last thing Pastor Dan said was, "I know it seems dark now, because we all loved Bernice, and we're going to miss her, but the best thing we can do when we're surrounded by darkness is to let our light, our love, our *goodness* shine! Let it light up the dark!"

After that, a few other people got up and told stories about how Grandma Bernice had made their lives a little easier, or a little nicer, or a little brighter. As I listened, I began to understand why Grandma had always said, "You should always leave a place nicer than you found it."

I remembered the last time Grandma Bernice had said that to me, the last time she would *ever* say that to me. It had been last Sunday, when Grandma wanted me to help pick up the Lanhams' trash and I hadn't wanted to. I could still hear the shock and disappointment in her voice as she said, "Lula Bell!" I had disappointed Grandma Bernice on her last day on earth. And now, I'd never get the chance to make it up to her. This thought caused fresh tears to fill my eyes and spill down my cheeks.

Mama handed me a handkerchief with a lavender-colored "B" and little flowers sewn onto it. The handkerchief had belonged to Grandma Bernice. It seemed somehow wrong to wipe my face on it.

"She'd want you to have it," Mama whispered, her breath warm on my ear, "and to *use* it."

The handkerchief didn't really help, seeing as how it smelled like Grandma Bernice's hand lotion, Rose Milk. This made me cry even more. So of course I used the handkerchief. I *had* to.

When the service was done, Pastor Dan came over carrying the biggest, most magnificent flower arrangement I'd ever seen: antique white roses, pale pink peonies, periwinkle blue hydrangea—some of the blossoms were as big as a cereal bowl. Pastor handed the flowers to Mama and kissed her on the cheek.

Mama looked at Pastor Dan, a question on her face. But he only patted her arm, promised to pray for us, and stepped back into the crowd.

Great Uncle Cleburne and Cousin Ethel lingered in front of Grandma Bernice's casket—saying good-bye, I guessed. That's when I heard Great Uncle Cleburne say, "They never get the lips right. Have you noticed that, Ethel?"

I wanted to march up there and slam the lid shut on the casket, to cover Grandma Bernice up and protect her from all these people who kept judging the way she looked. The truth was that Grandma didn't look her best. But if being *dead* isn't a good excuse for not looking your best, then I don't know what is.

Saying Good-bye

When we were back in the limo, Mama opened the little envelope sticking out of the flowers. She read the card, then pressed it to her chest and closed her eyes.

"What is it?" Daddy whispered.

It took her a minute, but finally Mama opened her teary eyes and handed the card to Daddy. He read it, smiled, and passed the card to me.

With her own hand, Grandma had written: *Being part of your family has been the greatest pleasure and privilege of my life. Thank you. All my love forever, Mama/Grandma Bernice*

I whispered, "She really knew how to light up the dark, didn't she?"

Mama smiled, a real smile, through her tears. "She did."

When the limo began moving, I looked out the window. Cars pulled over now, and people took pause when they saw us coming. That's because we were part of a long line of cars, a funeral procession, with police escorts at the front and back. I sent *Thank you, thank you, thank you,* thoughts to all the people who paused in honor of Grandma Bernice.

The graveside service was short, but still, it was the hardest part for me. It was hard because when it was over, we were all supposed to walk away and leave Grandma Bernice there, outside, in the drizzle, in a wooden box. Oh, it was a grand box— dark, polished wood with gold trim; it looked like a gigantic jewelry box. But the way I see it, a box is still a box. It just felt wrong to leave her there like that. So I didn't. I stayed right where I was, sitting on a metal folding chair beside Grandma Bernice, both of us protected by a green canopy with the words "White House Funeral Home" printed on it.

At first, everyone was very patient with me. Mama said, "Take your time, sweetheart." But as time wore on, even Daddy began to lose patience. "Time to go, Lula Bell," he finally said.

"No!" I said, shaking my head violently.

A gravedigger in overalls waited nearby, ready to collect the chairs and things, ready to lay Grandma Bernice to rest in the cold, wet ground. I gave him dirty looks and wished—hard—that he'd go away.

Mama, Daddy, Great Uncle Cleburne, and Cousin Ethel stood off to the side in the wet grass, having a quiet conversation. I couldn't hear what they were saying. When they finished talking, Mama and Cousin Ethel got into the limo and it drove away, leaving Daddy, Great Uncle Cleburne, Grandma Bernice, and me—and the gravedigger.

The gravedigger started toward Daddy and Great Uncle Cleburne. "Anything I can do?" he called out.

There was another quiet conversation that I couldn't quite make out. Then the man, who was enormous, came over, ducked under the tent, and folded himself into the chair beside mine. I ignored him and stared straight ahead.

"Name's Jimmy," he said.

I scrunched up my face and gave him my meanest, scariest look. Mr. Jimmy smiled. I looked away. For a while, Mr. Jimmy and I sat side by side in silence.

"So," he said, finally.

I continued to stare straight ahead as I said in a small voice, "It just seems so . . . so . . ."

"Final?" Mr. Jimmy guessed.

I lowered my head and nodded.

"It ain't," Mr. Jimmy said.

"How do you know?" I risked a quick glance at him.

He moved his huge shoulders up and down. "Just do."

"But *how*?"

Mr. Jimmy was quiet for so long that I decided he wasn't going to answer me. But then he did. "At night, when it's dark, how do you know mornin's comin'? In the wintertime, when everything's dead, how do you know it ain't? How do you know spring's comin'?"

I looked at him.

Mr. Jimmy stood and let his eyes wander over Grandma Bernice's casket. "She ain't here, but she ain't gone neither." Then he looked at me.

I nodded.

He laid a hand on top of Grandma's casket. "She ain't *here*," he said again.

I stood. If Grandma wasn't here, then I figured there was no reason for me to be here. So I turned and walked away, despite feeling awkward and uneasy and . . . just all wrong.

We were almost home by the time I realized why. I hadn't said good-bye to Grandma at the cemetery—because she hadn't been there. I would never get to tell her good-bye. Or anything else.

A Pity Party

There *was* a party going on at home, if you ask me. It was definitely a sad party, but still. There were people everywhere. They sat and stood around, eating and talking in low, respectful tones.

I found Mama in the kitchen. "Where did all this food come from?" I asked.

Honestly, if I hadn't known what our counters and table looked like, I never would've been able to figure it out today; you couldn't even see them. Our whole kitchen was *buried* in food: sandwich platters, Jell-O molds, fruit salads, tossed salads, cakes, pies, casseroles, casseroles, and more casseroles.

"Didn't you hear the doorbell ringing like crazy?" Mama asked, pulling another casserole out of the refrigerator.

"Yes, ma'am," I said.

"Well," Mama said, as if this answered my question.

"Well, what?"

Mama bent to slide the casserole into the oven and then stood. "People bring food when someone . . . passes."

"Why" was the word that popped into my head and out of my mouth. It just didn't make sense to me that when people heard that Grandma Bernice had died, they thought to themselves, *Oh! In that case, the Bonners must be ready to eat. I better get over there with my vegetable medley right away!*

"That's just the way it is, Lula Bell," Mama said, "the way it's always been—people are just trying to be helpful and supportive is all."

I shook my head in disgust.

Mama put a hand on her hip. "Lula Bell, can you imagine us having to *make* all this food to feed all these people after the funeral?"

I shrugged. I knew she had me there; I just wasn't ready to give in.

"Why, you could hardly get out of bed yesterday."

Just because I hadn't gotten out of bed didn't mean I couldn't.

Mama grabbed a small bunch of red pin-cushion roses off the counter and handed them to me. "I found these on the front porch when we got home," she said as she hurried out of the kitchen.

The tiny, delicate roses were tied together with a string attached to a shiny red ribbon, and not the usual kind. The rectangular ribbon had gold lettering that read "Second Place Science Fair." I'd forgotten all about the science fair at school. That seemed like ages ago. I stood there, trying to figure how long it had really been. Only days, I realized.

"Uncle Cleburne . . . some more sweet tea?" I heard Mama say in the next room.

I took the red ribbon off the roses and put them in a jar of water.

When Mama came back, I thought about telling her that Alan and I had won second place at the school science fair. But what difference did it make? None. It didn't make me feel any better, so it probably wouldn't make Mama feel any better either. I dropped the ribbon into the junk drawer and closed it.

When I turned, Mama handed me a plate. "You *have* to eat, Lula Bell," she said, raising her eyebrows at me. Then she grabbed the big pitcher of sweet tea and was gone again.

By her eyebrows and the tone of her voice, I knew Mama meant business. I chose one of the few casseroles I thought I recognized (chicken, I hoped) and spooned some onto my plate. Have you ever noticed how all casseroles look the same from a distance? They all look brown and toasty and yummy, without a hint of the grossness lurking beneath the crust. (If you cook, here's a little tip for you: *good* food doesn't have to be disguised.)

Sitting on the stairs with my plate in my lap, watching the pitiful little party in our living room, I couldn't help remembering Grandma Bernice's birthday party. All the same people had been there, plus Grandma Bernice. I remembered how she'd wanted me to sing, how hopeful she'd looked when she'd asked about my song for the school talent show and how I'd disappointed her. For the second time. On her last day on earth.

Just then Mrs. Purdy—who is the snazziest dresser I know—walked past. Her leopard-print high heels caught my eye, and I was instantly back in the hallway at school, Grandma Bernice waving at me like mad, in her leopard-trimmed sweat suit. *No! No! No!* my mind screamed. *Get out of here! It's too much!* And it was. It was like looking at the worst, ugliest photo of myself, a picture I wanted to tear into a million tiny pieces, burn, and bury. Only it was too late. Someone else had already seen the picture, and that someone had been Grandma Bernice. It had hurt her. *I* had hurt her. And now Grandma would never know how sorry I was. Tears burned behind my eyes, so I closed them.

Mama cleared her throat. When I opened my eyes, she was standing right in front of me, holding a stack of dirty dishes.

I wanted to confess to her. I wanted tell her how I wished I'd never, ever hurt or disappointed Grandma Bernice. But most of all . . .

"I just wish I hadn't fallen asleep," I blurted out.

"Lula Bell, honey," Mama said ever so softly, "Grandma Bernice didn't die because you fell asleep."

I thought about this and knew that it was true. But still, I couldn't help wishing that things had gone differently somehow.

"Now please eat something," Mama said. "Please."

I picked up my fork and used it to push casserole lumps around on my plate.

"Thank you," Mama said as she started moving again.

I must've been concentrating really hard on rearranging my lumps so that they'd look like I'd eaten, because when I glanced up, I was startled to find Great Uncle Cleburne—and his walker—standing right in front of me. Great Uncle Cleburne's watery blue eyes were soft and understanding, just like Grandma Bernice's had been.

"Aw, I know how you feel, hon'," Great Uncle Cleburne said. "Really, I do, but you gotta eat—you gotta take care of yourself."

I just blinked at him.

"If Bernice were here right now, she'd go out of her way to care for you, wouldn't she?"

I thought about this and nodded.

"Taking care of you was important to Bernice, so the best thing you can do for her right now is take care of yourself."

"You look a lot like her," I said. "You have the same eyes."

Great Uncle Cleburne smiled. "Thank you, darlin'. That helps."

I was confused, and I guess it showed.

Uncle Cleburne explained, "It helps to know I've got a little piece of my baby sister with me all the time—somethin' I can see in the mirror, on my very own face, any old time I want."

I nodded my understanding.

"Now, if you'll excuse me, I gotta get some more sweet tea. Your mama makes the best sweet tea I ever tasted!"

"The trick is not to be afraid of the sugar. You just gotta dump it in there—while the tea's still good and hot," I said.

"I knew it!" Great Uncle Cleburne said to himself as he started off sloooowly. "I *knew* Ethel was bein' stingy with the sugar!"

I took a bite of chicken—just chicken—and forced myself to swallow. *Grandma Bernice, I hope you're watching*, I thought. *I'm trying. I'm trying to take care of myself. For you.*

We put Great Uncle Cleburne on the fold-out sofa bed downstairs for the night.

"Have you taken your medication?" Cousin Ethel asked him.

"I've taken it," Great Uncle Cleburne said.

"Lula Bell, get him some water," Mama said to me, and then to Great Uncle Cleburne, "just in case you get thirsty."

Cousin Ethel knelt and tucked the sheets and blankets in way too tight, under the mattress. "We can't have you falling outta bed," she said.

Great Uncle Cleburne held onto the sheets with both hands and stared at the ceiling without blinking.

"Um, can you move your feet?" I asked, because Cousin Ethel was pulling and tucking everything so tight that Great Uncle Cleburne's toes were pointing like a ballerina's under the covers.

Great Uncle Cleburne didn't bother to answer me.

"Now then." Cousin Ethel stood. "You sure you don't need to use the bathroom, Daddy?"

All of a sudden, Great Uncle Cleburne started waving his arms and saying, "Shoo! Shoo! Shoo, flies, *shoo*!"

I was pretty sure that *we* were the flies he was referring to. I could kind of see his point, the way everybody was buzzing around him.

We all said our goodnights and headed for the stairs. Mama led the way; Cousin Ethel and Daddy followed, while I brought up the rear.

On the landing, I noticed that Grandma Bernice's grandfather clock had stopped. It stood as still and as silent as a statue. At first, I thought that even that old clock had enough sense to stop and mourn Grandma Bernice. But then I remembered that Grandma had been the only one to wind it. So of course it stopped. I left it that way.

Upstairs, Cousin Ethel disappeared into Grandma Bernice's bedroom and closed the door. Mama smoothed my hair, kissed my forehead, and headed for her bedroom.

But Daddy hung back in the hallway. "You okay?" he asked me.

I nodded.

"Want me to tuck you in?"

I shook my head.

"I promise I'll do it just like Cousin Ethel," Daddy whispered, teasing me.

I smiled and shook my head again.

"All right then. See you in the mornin'," Daddy said.

"See you in the mornin'," I echoed, my hand on my bedroom doorknob.

Daddy continued to watch me without moving. I think he was waiting for me to change my mind.

I slipped into my bedroom and shut the door quietly behind me. I hadn't been in here in days, I suddenly realized. When I learned that Grandma Bernice was gone, I'd gone straight to her room and stayed there. I hadn't bathed, hadn't changed clothes, hadn't even brushed my hair or teeth, not until this morning.

For a minute, I just stood there in the dark, breathing deeply. Then, I reached over and flipped on the light.

What I saw caused me to sink to my knees. For the last time, Grandma Bernice had left my room nicer than she'd found it. For the last time, she'd straightened my bed and folded my covers back neatly. For the last time, she'd left one of her raspberry chocolates on my pillow. Tears streaked down my cheeks.

I had nothing left in me, no more tears, nothing, by the time I got up off the floor. My eyeballs felt tired and achy. My body felt heavy, and it took all my strength just to make it to the bed. Gently, I picked up the pink-foiled chocolate and placed it on my nightstand. Then, still wearing my funeral dress and lacy socks, I pulled back the rosebud quilt that Grandma Bernice had made for me and climbed into bed.

It Has to Get Better— Right?

I thought it would get better after the funeral—mostly because I didn't see how things could get any worse. But I was wrong. It was *much* worse.

After the funeral, everybody went back to their normal lives—which seemed unfair, considering the fact that I couldn't go back to my normal life (normal life = life with Grandma Bernice). Even Daddy had to go back to work.

"But what if I *need* you, Daddy? I don't even know where you are half the time," I pleaded.

"I'll call to check on y'all every night, like always," Daddy said. "Tomorrow we'll be in Oklahoma City, and after that, we move on to Wichita, Kansas—you can always check the Boots and Whistles website to see where I am."

Check the website? Like any other stranger? "Um ... I'm your *daughter*," I informed him, teary-eyed.

"Guess that makes you pretty lucky, hunh?" Daddy said, grinning.

"No, it makes *you* lucky," I teased back, but my heart wasn't in it.

There was nothing more anybody could do, I guess. Soon, the doorbell and phone stopped ringing, and Mama and I were left alone. Mostly, I stayed in bed. But that morning, when I woke up, I realized there was someone beside me.

The person beside me sniffed. I knew that sniff; it was Mama's.

I turned over to face her.

"She was right," Mama said, crying softly into my other pillow.

"Huh?"

"I should've made her lobster soup. I should've made it for her *every night*," Mama cried.

"But you did make her lobster soup, Mama."

She sniffed again and nodded.

"Grandma got everything she wanted," I said,

trying my best to comfort Mama. "She got lobster soup; she got a birthday party; she got to see her brother, Cleburne . . ." I hesitated, not sure whether I should go on.

Mama nodded again, but she didn't seem very comforted.

I thought maybe I should share my secret: "Grandma Bernice even died the way she wanted. She—"

"I don't wanna talk about that," Mama interrupted, squeezing her eyes shut.

I closed my mouth and waited.

When Mama's eyes fluttered open, she said, "Grandma's in a better place now. That's what we need to focus on."

That's when I realized I'd been wrong. All this time, I thought I'd been crying for Grandma Bernice, but suddenly I realized I hadn't been crying for her at all. After all, Grandma had gotten everything she wanted, and everyone said that she was in a better place, that she was happy. So, why cry for her when she wouldn't have cried for herself? I didn't. I cried for *me*. I cried because I'd never see Grandma again for the rest of my life—and already, I missed her. So, the way I figured, I was only feeling sorry for myself.

This made me feel a little better, because there's a strict limit to how long you're allowed to feel sorry for yourself in our house. People who exceed this limit—or complain—are punished with extra chores. "Feeling sorry for yourself never accomplishes anything," Mama always says, "while hard work always brings accomplishment."

My biggest and best accomplishment these days was getting out of bed. Sometimes, I wandered into Grandma Bernice's bedroom, like I did late that morning. I studied the framed photos on her nightstand and tried to guess what Grandma had seen in them. There was one of Mama laughing with her head thrown back, a picture of me sleeping with my head on Daddy's chest when I was two or three years old, a picture of Grandma Bernice and Papa Roy on their wedding day—they looked so young and beautiful and happy. I put the pictures back exactly the way they had been.

I ran my hands over the lavender quilt on Grandma's bed as if I were touching Grandma's hands rather than just the tiny stitches her hands had once made.

I picked up Grandma's old, beat-up Bible and remembered her teaching me about Bible cracking.

Bible cracking is something you do when you need help. It's when you pick up the Bible and let it fall open, so it can speak to you in the first scripture you lay eyes on. Grandma's Bible fell open to Hebrews, and the first scripture I laid eyes on was highlighted in yellow. It read, "Faith is the substance of things hoped for."

I'd had faith, hadn't I? Hadn't I hoped and prayed that Grandma Bernice would be okay, that God would give her back, that He would fix all this somehow? But He didn't, did He?

When I looked up, I saw the wreath of dried flowers from Grandma's garden: hydrangeas, which had once been a vibrant purplish-blue but were so faded I could barely make out the color. *Dead, dead, dead*, I thought. And then I cried some more—for myself.

I was holding Grandma Bernice's slippers when Mama came upstairs and said, "Lula Bell, come down and have some breakfast."

I hugged the slippers to me protectively and said, "No, thank you."

Later, when Mama came upstairs again, I was looking at Grandma's glasses, trying to picture the exact way her face twisted and bunched when she had wanted to move her glasses up without using her hands. I could picture it mostly but not exactly. I would've given anything I had to see her do it again.

"Lula Bell, honey," Mama said, "won't you eat just a little somethin' for lunch?"

"Maybe later," I said. (I figured "maybe later" sounded better than the truth, which was that I had no desire to ever swallow another bite of food—and even less desire to swallow the food we had, which was still mostly casseroles.)

I must've fallen asleep in Grandma Bernice's room, because the next thing I knew there was a hand on my shoulder. I heard Mama murmur, "Lula Bell . . . Lula . . ."

I opened my eyes. Grandma's lace curtains were twilight blue, the color of evening. As quickly as the time of day came to me, so did the memory: Grandma Bernice was gone.

Mama didn't say whatever she'd come to say. Instead, she cuddled up next to me on Grandma Bernice's bed, and we cried together. This time, I cried some for Mama, too, because, after all, Grandma Bernice was my mama's mama. I suddenly realized that both my mama's mama *and* daddy were dead, and that Mama was practically an orphan now. An orphan! How awful! After that, I did all my crying for Mama.

"I'm so sorry," I managed in between sobs.

"I know. I am, too," Mama said.

After a little while, Mama let out a deep sigh and got up, wearing a determined look on her face. This is almost never good news for me. "It'd do you good to get out of the house," Mama said.

"No, thanks. Maybe later," I said, as if she'd asked me about eating again.

"But Lula Bell, this is your last lesson, your last chance to practice before the talent show auditions," Mama reminded me. "And Mrs. West is expecting you."

I knew then that it was Thursday, because Mrs. West gives me piano and voice lessons on Thursdays. *Thursday. Without Grandma Bernice.* I didn't want to go anywhere, especially not on a Thursday, and especially not to the Wests' house.

"You know how important the talent show was to Grandma," Mama added.

I nodded to indicate that I knew the talent show was important to Grandma, *not* that I was willing to get up and leave the house, but Mama must've misunderstood.

"Good," she said. "Get cleaned up and come downstairs for a bite of supper before you leave. It'll help you to get out—you'll see."

For a few miserable minutes, I just lay there, feeling lonelier than I ever had before. *Mama just doesn't know,* I thought. *She doesn't know what she's asking me to do or how hard it is. She just doesn't know.* Even if I'd wanted to—which I didn't—I wasn't sure I could do what Mama was asking.

The Show Must Go On

When I arrived at the Wests' house, Mrs. West ushered me to the baby grand piano, where she already had my sheet music in place.

The show must go on, I thought sadly, because Mrs. West had been saying that as long as I'd known her: "Oh, you have a cold? Well, I'm sorry to hear it, but the show must go on!" "Oh, your arm has broken off? Well, I'm so sorry, but thank heaven you have another one, because the show must go on!"

Okay, okay, maybe I'm exaggerating. I'd had allergies, not a cold, and neither of my arms has ever broken off—it was just a sprain. And Mrs. West hadn't been cranky or mean on either occasion—she's never really mean. She always listens and gives me sympathy—right before she says, "The show must go on!" She would know, I guess. Mrs. West used to be a singer—she even performed at the Grand Ole Opry before Alan was born. Her dad had been a famous musician, too—a piano player.

I sat down on the bench and stared at the musical notes on the paper in front of me. Mrs. West perched on the end of the piano bench, waiting. Obediently, I played the first few bars of "Under the Boardwalk" and then stopped abruptly.

"That's all right," Mrs. West said kindly. "Just start again."

I wrung my hands.

After a time, Mrs. West turned and looked at me.

"I can't do it," I told her.

"Okaaaay," Mrs. West said slowly, in a way that seemed to ask why.

I didn't know what to say. So I just sat there, trying to sort it all out in my head.

Music had always been a way of celebrating at our house. The second we had something to celebrate, big or small, Grandma Bernice took to the piano. Piano playing and singing marked happy times—birthdays, holidays, even snow days. On snowy, winter nights when we learned that school had been canceled the next day, Grandma Bernice would sit down at the piano and bang out "Midnight Hour" while I danced around the living room for joy. To me, "Midnight Hour" would always mean "stay up late, snow day tomorrow," while "Here Comes the Sun" would always mean "first day of spring." "Summertime" would always mean . . . well, "summertime."

"Lula Bell?" Mrs. West said softly.

"I don't want to play any music," I blurted out, "because I don't want to *hear* any music."

"Is there a reason . . . aside from the obvious?" Mrs. West asked.

I tried to think how to explain.

Mrs. West made huffy, impatient sounds.

I checked the stairs—just to make sure that Alan wasn't sitting at the top, listening in, the way he usually did—and then confessed, "You know how sometimes when you hear an old song, it takes you back to a certain time and place, whether you want it to or not?"

"Yes," Mrs. West said.

"Well, I never want to come back to *this* time, *this* place in my life again," I said, and I meant it. I didn't want to mark this time with the song "Under the Boardwalk"—or *any* song—because then, whenever I heard "Under the Boardwalk," no matter where I was, it would always take me back to the worst, saddest time of my life.

Mrs. West put her arm around me and gave me a little squeeze. "Do you want to know why I think that happens, why music bypasses all our defenses and goes straight to the soul?"

"Why?"

Mrs. West smiled. "I think music is where heaven meets the earth."

What was that supposed to mean? It probably meant that we were having a music lesson today, whether I wanted to or not.

"Now then," Mrs. West said, nodding at the sheet music, "the show must go on."

Yep, just as I'd thought. "I'm not singing," I informed her.

"All right," Mrs. West said easily. "Just play."

I sighed heavily, checked the stairs again, and played. The whole song. It hurt me to do it. I could feel the vibration of each note inside me, creating tiny cracks in my heart, cracks that would break open some sunshiney day when I least expected it.

"Very good," Mrs. West said when I finished. "Again, and this time, sing."

I played up to the point where I was supposed to start singing, then stopped. "I *can't* sing. I just can't. *Please*," I begged. "It isn't in me."

"It's in you. It's always in you," Mrs. West said with certainty. "Find it."

It was hard, maybe one of the hardest things I've ever done. But the next time around, I found my voice and came in singing on the second verse.

That night, I learned the one good thing about being forced to sing and play the piano at the same time: doing it takes every ounce of my concentration. There isn't enough room left in my brain to hold another thought, not a single one. So, for a few minutes here and there, I forgot about Grandma Bernice; I forgot how sad and lonely I was; I forgot my own name. For a few minutes, there was only music.

By the end of the lesson, I didn't want to stop, even though I had never wanted to start. I also didn't want to go home, which was weird because I hadn't wanted to leave home in the first place.

I checked the stairs again. There was still no sign of Alan. By now, I'd checked the stairs about fifty-two million times; usually, I was mad at Alan for spying on me, but for some weird reason, tonight, I was sort of mad at Alan for *not* spying on me. I figured all this meant that I was pretty messed up. For a second, I pictured my insides like a compass spinning round and round, out of control, instead of steadily pointing north.

Mrs. West rose from the piano bench, smoothed her skirt, and then hollered at the ceiling, "Alan! Alan, Lula Bell's about to go! Come down and walk her out!"

Before she'd even finished, Alan appeared at the top of the stairs. The sight of him, or more specifically the sight of his hair, made me smile just a little.

I met Alan at the front door, where he shoved his hands deep in his pockets and studied his feet. An awkward silence passed between us.

"Thanks for the roses and the ribbon," I offered.

"You're welcome," Alan said, meeting my eyes. "I'm sorry it wasn't a blue ribbon—I had trouble with the humidifier."

"Well, don't tell my mama that," I said. "When I explained our tornado box to her, she said we ought to take an extra fan and an extra humidifier to school as backups. Can you believe that?"

Alan smiled his crooked smile. "She was right."

"Yeah, that's why I said *don't tell her.*"

Alan and I laughed nervous little laughs, and then came another silence—this one so long and uncomfortable that my toes began feeling their way around inside my shoes.

This time, Alan was the one to speak. "The funeral was nice."

I nodded.

"I'm sorry about Grandma Bernice," he said. "I really liked her."

"Me, too," I said, looking down.

"I know. She was your best friend."

She was? I thought about it, and after a minute, I realized that Alan was right: Grandma Bernice had been my best friend. I wished I'd known it sooner so that I could've told Grandma. I felt my chin quiver.

"Igottago," I barked just before I yanked the front door open and leapt out into the night.

I stood on the Wests' front porch, gulping at the cool night air. It helped.

I still didn't want to go home, but I started walking and as I did, the sky started sprinkling again—it had rained on and off all day. So I hurried along our quiet, tree-lined street.

I cut through our yard and around back, the soft ground sinking under my feet, the wet grass licking at my ankles. When I reached our back door, I stopped and tried to brace myself for what I'd find inside. Or rather what and who I wouldn't find.

Mama had left a small lamp on in the kitchen, but it didn't feel all that welcoming to me. The whole house felt dark and empty, sad and strange.

As I took my jacket off, I noticed a box of Krispy Kreme doughnuts sitting on the kitchen table. That's when I realized that Mama had known that asking me to leave the house, to play the piano, to sing, was asking a lot. And asking me to come back home and face Grandma Bernice's absence in a new way was asking even more. Mama considered the fact that I'd actually done all of it, a real accomplishment. I was grateful then for the doughnuts I would never eat, because they let me know that I wasn't quite as alone as I'd thought.

Next to the doughnuts on the table was the *White House Watch*, still in its plastic sleeve. My shoes squished as I walked over to the table and sat down, just like I would have if Grandma Bernice had been there. As I sat there remembering the last time I'd had doughnuts with my obituaries, I couldn't help wishing that I'd known it would be my last Thursday night with Grandma Bernice. I would've said more important things. Things like "I'm sorry," and "I love you, Grandma Bernice," and "You're my best friend."

"Lula Bell?" Mama said, flicking on the overhead light. "Honey, what're you doing? Why are you just sitting here in the dark?"

I blinked back my tears and shrugged.

"I was waiting for you in the living room."

I wanted to tell her that she was supposed to wait for me in the kitchen, like Grandma Bernice always had, but I didn't—after all, Mama was an orphan now.

I think Mama wanted to tell me that I should've taken off my squishy shoes at the door, because I saw her frown at the muddy brown water I'd tracked across the floor. But instead, she smiled and didn't say a thing.

Hitting the Limit

The birds outside my window were singing when I apparently reached the limit to how long I'd be allowed to stay home, feeling sorry for myself.

"Time to get up," Mama said cheerfully as she drew back my curtains. A pale pink sky was giving way to a beautiful, bright blue Monday morning.

"Whyyyy?" I moaned.

"You've gotta get ready for school, Lula Bell," Mama said, as if I should've known. "C'mon now or you'll be late."

As if to prove her point, Grandma Bernice's old

grandfather clock rang out in song and then gonged six times, announcing that it was 6 o'clock.

I pulled the covers up over my head. How could Mama expect me to just go on back to school now, like I'd only been sick with the flu or something? The *flu* hadn't come to our house; *death* had come to our house, and it had taken one of us away—forever.

"The talent show auditions are today," Mama announced. She obviously expected this to make a huge difference.

It made a difference all right: it made me want to stay home from school even more. Why, oh why had I fantasized about the talent show, out loud, in front of Mama and Grandma Bernice? I'll tell you why: because the day that little slip of yellow paper about the fifth grade talent show came home from school, the talent show was so far off, it seemed like it would never come. So, fantasizing about being in the talent show was like fantasizing about what I might want for Christmas. I know Christmas will come eventually, but it's usually so far off when I start talking about what I want that I know I have plenty of time to change my mind, again and again, which I always do. But when I changed my mind about the talent show, Mama and Grandma Bernice acted like I'd changed my mind about college—and said I wasn't going. They both said that I would be in the talent show, and that was all there was to it.

Mama sighed. "C'mon, Lula Bell, there's work to be done."

I didn't move.

Mama sat down on the edge of my bed and placed a gentle hand on my back. "Lula Bell, if staying home feeling sorry would bring Grandma Bernice back, I would do it. I would do it no matter how long it took. But it won't bring her back—it won't *do* anything."

I knew this speech. It was a slightly softer version of Mama's "Feeling sorry for yourself never accomplishes anything, while hard work always brings accomplishment" speech.

"Okay, okay," I whimpered from under the covers, even though it was definitely *not* okay with me.

I felt really mad at Mama, not tired-mad but mad-mad, but what could I do? It's not like you can haul off and start yelling at your mama. Well, you can, I guess, but I wouldn't. I figure there's a reason that for all the times I've seen mamas yelling at their kids in the grocery store, I've never once seen a kid yelling at their mama. So, I stomped around the house, slamming things and huffing, but I didn't yell. And I didn't complain—because that would've resulted in extra chores.

I decided to wear my lucky orange T-shirt to school because of the auditions. Now, I admit that my lucky T-shirt had gotten a little smallish and tightish over the winter, but when I looked at myself in the bathroom mirror, I thought I could get away with it this once. Oh sure, I knew I could've gotten away with it a lot easier if my hair had been curly and blond . . . and maybe if my eyes had been pale blue, but you've got to work with what you have. In my case, that was plain, boring brown eyes and straight, boring brown hair. I tried putting my hair into a ponytail but ended up with more of a pony*stub*, so I took it down. I thought about asking Mama to curl my hair with the curling iron, but I figured I'd have to ask *nicely*, which might make Mama think I wasn't mad at her anymore, which I was. The curls would just fall out in an hour or two anyway, so I left my hair the same as always.

When I came downstairs, Mama set her coffee cup down and said, "You're not wearing *that* old shirt, are you?"

I froze. I needed to rethink the whole shirt thing. I had a hard enough time fitting in at school—I couldn't afford to wear the wrong clothes, too.

"But I *need* it for the auditions," I decided out loud. "It's my lucky shirt."

"Oh," Mama said.

I made a huffy sound and dropped into a chair at the kitchen table.

"What makes that shirt lucky?" Mama asked as she pulled a gallon of milk from the refrigerator.

"I won it," I said. *Duh.*

Mama smiled and shook her head. "You didn't win that shirt. We paid for it by buying more than ten boxes of cereal, which no one ate."

"It wasn't good cereal, Mama," I said, trying to defend myself and my lucky shirt.

"Well, I hope you'll remember that the next time you see a commercial on TV promising prizes if you buy a bazillion boxes of cereal. When food's good, eating it is the reward."

"Hmph!" I said.

Mama slid my breakfast onto the table in front of me, just like Grandma Bernice used to do. It wasn't the right person, and it wasn't the right breakfast. It was cereal—*cold* cereal!

"Um, is this about my shirt?" I asked.

"What?" Mama stopped moving and turned to look at me.

I glanced down at my cereal.

"Oh. No, of course not. I just don't have enough time to fix you a hot breakfast. I have to finish getting ready for work."

That's when I knew that nothing was ever going to be okay again. Not even breakfast.

"But don't worry," Mama said on her way out of the kitchen. "I'll be here when you get home from school."

It was all too much, too early in the morning. I wanted to go back to bed. I *wanted* to forget. But I was stuck remembering instead, remembering my last normal breakfast: how Grandma Bernice had cooked for me, how she smiled as soon as she saw me, how she sat down at the table with me, how she got so excited over the red cardinal that perched on our hummingbird feeder—and the white hummingbird argument that followed.

"Lula Bell, you haven't even touched your cereal," Mama said when she came back into the kitchen.

I burst into tears.

Mama sat down at the table beside me and

waited. When I began to quiet, she said, "We have to go on living, Lula Bell."

I nodded.

"We have to go on living for Grandma Bernice, *in honor* of Grandma Bernice, because she never wasted a day in her life."

I wanted to say something like, *Nuh-uh, remember the time that Grandma Bernice stayed in bed for a month?* Only I couldn't, because Mama was right: I only knew of one day that Grandma Bernice had failed to get out of bed, and it was the day she died. Since I was—slightly inconveniently—alive that day, I wiped my face with my napkin, took a deep breath, and pushed back from the table.

WARNING! DANGER ZONE!

When I got down to my bus stop, I was mighty relieved to see that Kali Keele wasn't there yet. But Alan West was. He was crouched down on the bank of Honey Run Creek, skipping stones across the water.

As soon as he heard me, Alan stood and wiped his hands on his pants. "Good morning, Lula Bell," he said brightly.

"Hey." I slipped out of my heavy backpack and let it fall at my feet. "Thanks for dropping off my make-up work," I said, not that I'd done any of it.

"I was glad to do it," Alan said. "It was no trouble at all. None whatsoever."

I barely heard him. I wasn't really listening. "Have you ever heard of a white hummingbird?" I asked.

"There have been reported sightings of white, or albino, hummingbirds," Alan said, "but if they exist, they're very rare."

"*If* they exist?" I repeated.

"Well, there's no proof yet. No one's ever photographed an albino hummingbird that I know of."

I nodded.

Alan grinned at me.

"What?" I said.

"I'm still undefeated," he said, puffing out his chest a little.

"At what?" I asked, because Alan isn't exactly athletic, if you know what I mean.

"Your questions. You've never once stumped me, Lula Bell."

He was right, but then I figure it's pretty hard to stump somebody who reads every single thing he can get his hands on—from books to bubble gum wrappers, and everything in between. In addition to this, each morning Alan checks the local weather forecast and national defense readiness condition (DEFCON), which is reported on a scale of one to five, one meaning we're at war and five meaning we're at peace. In fact, the only thing I knew of that Alan wasn't interested in was sports. For a second, I was tempted to ask Alan about last night's sports scores, just to prove that I *could* stump him anytime I wanted, but I forgot all that when I heard the bus.

Immediately, I began sending thoughts to our bus driver: *Hurry! Hurry! Hurry! Hurry and get here before Kali comes!*

As the bus squealed to a stop in front of Alan and me, I looked around. No Kali. I hefted my backpack onto my back, climbed on, and took a seat. Alan sat down beside me.

I ignored him and looked out the window. That's when I saw Kali Keele running toward the bus, her blond ponytail and perfect pink ribbon whipping in the wind behind her. My heart started pounding. *No! No! No!* I thought, and then, *Go! Go! Go!*

The bus lurched forward as I continued to watch Kali chasing after us. She grew smaller and smaller in the window, as my sense of relief grew bigger and bigger. *Phew!*

As soon as I walked into my classroom, everybody stopped what they were doing and stared at me. There were a few whispers, but nobody said anything *to* me. Well, I was used to that, used to being mostly invisible, so it was the collective staring that was new—and bothersome.

I hurried to my desk, where I sat down and tried to make myself invisible again. Was Mama right? Had I made a mistake in wearing this shirt? Or maybe I had something stuck to me. A sock from the dryer? Or worse, a pair of panties? *Omigosh!* I thought, *I'll have to change schools if I've been walking around with panties stuck to me! We'll have to move!* I tried to search myself without being obvious but couldn't find a thing.

As soon as the second bell rang, Mrs. Pritchett stood up. "Lula Bell, sweetie pie, we're *so* glad you're back," she gushed, giving me the same sort of gooey look that everyone had given me at Grandma Bernice's funeral—like, *Awwww, poor little Lula Bell.*

I looked around. Nobody in my class seemed surprised. They all knew about Grandma Bernice, I realized. That's why they stared at me. As if I didn't have enough problems.

"Now," Mrs. Pritchett said, turning away from me, "I have exciting news, class! Very soon, we'll be going on a field trip to visit the home of Confederate hero Sam Davis!"

Kids smiled at each other and at Mrs. Pritchett. Field trips made everybody happy, everybody except me.

As Mrs. Pritchett handed out forms for our parents to sign, she said, "I'd like for all of you to choose a bus buddy. That's the person you'll sit with on the bus."

Kids paired off silently, either by exchanging looks and nods, pointing at one another, or urgently mouthing the words "You and me! You and me!"

I did none of these things. Instead, I stared into my lap, knowing that I'd end up being bus buddies with either Mrs. Pritchett or Alan West, both of whom I considered tuna when I really needed PB&J.

Sure enough, when asked, Alan said, "Lula Bell Bonner" and smiled at me.

I didn't smile back. Instead, I closed my eyes and thought, *Hopeless.*

Somehow I made it through the day at school. It wasn't easy. It was like trying to run in water that's waist high, but still, I kept putting one foot in front of the other and pushing. Since I'd made it that far, I kept right on pushing. After school, I headed for the gym to audition for the fifth grade talent show that would take place on the last day of school.

As soon as I walked into the gym, I saw Kali Keele and her friends off near the bleachers, practicing dance moves. They saw me, too, and exchanged looks and giggles. I realized then that all the kids in the gym sat or stood in little groups. Everyone had at least one friend with them. No one had come alone. Except for me.

I started to wring my hands and fidget, but I caught myself. *Stop it! Don't be weird!* I told myself. *Act like the others!* Of course, I had to look at the others a little more closely in order to know how to act like them. They all looked casual . . . and confident, I decided.

There was a long table set up near the stage, and when I walked over, thinking *casual and confident, casual and confident* over and over in my head, I found sign-up sheets and pens scattered on the table. Determined, I picked up a pen just as I overheard Kali say my name.

I turned around in time to see Kali demonstrating this strange sort of walk for her friends. Her back was straight but too stiff, and her arms didn't swing, didn't move at all. And even though Kali held her head high, her eyes cast around suspiciously and her mouth sort of grimaced.

When she finished her weird walk, Kali doubled over laughing. Her friends howled with laughter, too—all of them except for Emilou Meriweather, who'd been my friend last year. When Emilou saw me watching, she lowered her head, and her cheeks turned bright pink.

That's when I knew Kali was imitating me, the way I'd walked over to the table, trying to look casual and confident.

I felt my own cheeks heat up as I tried to swallow the lump in my throat but couldn't. Then I panicked, my thoughts spiraling out of control: *I don't want to be here. Nobody here likes me. Nobody wants to hear me sing. I don't want to sing. I can't do it. I can't play and I can't sing. Not for them. Even if I could, Kali and her friends would probably laugh me off the stage. After that, they'll just have another reason to make fun of me, another little tidbit they can use to torment and humiliate me.* I could just imagine Kali singing "Under the Boardwalk" on the bus. *Every day.* I could already hear the laughter that would follow. *Every day.* These images and sounds swirled in my brain until they became a single thought, a single word: *GO!*

My toes were already going wild inside my shoes and my feet were itching to run, but then I remembered what Alan had said about omega wolves and made myself stay put. I took a deep breath, laid the pen back down on the table as calmly as I could, considering my hand was trembling, and walked toward the door at what I hoped was a normal pace. But I didn't quite make it. (Here's a little tip for you: wiggling your toes while walking affects your balance. Apparently.)

When I was almost to the door, I stumbled and fell. Everybody laughed. Everybody, not just Kali and her crew. I forgot about wolves then, scrambled to my feet and out the door, the sound of laughter fading with every step, pushing me on, despite my throbbing knee.

Outside, I watched my bus pull away and turn onto the street—without me. *Naturally.* I thought about going back inside to call Mama from the office, but how could I? No, the fresh air tasted like freedom, and the sunshine felt warm and safe. So I started walking.

As I walked, the whole gym scene replayed over and over in my mind. At first, I was mad at myself for trying so hard to look casual and confident, for being so fidgety, for having such squirmy toes, and especially for falling. But that just made me feel worse. So then I tried being mad at Kali. I heard her say my name, saw her doing her weird walk, saw her doubled over laughing. I saw Kali's friends laughing—I could still hear them, too—and I saw Emilou Meriweather lower her head in shame. It was easier, and much more satisfying, to be mad at Kali.

For the millionth time, I wondered why I'd ever been friends with her. See, in third grade, Kali Keele and I were BFFs—best friends forever—for two entire months. During those months, we'd been inseparable at school, and we'd spent time together outside of school, too—at my house. But the more time Kali spent with me, the less she seemed to like me, until finally, I guess she decided that she flat-out hated me—and everyone related to me.

The last time Kali had been at my house had been on a Thursday. So Kali had been there with Grandma Bernice and me when we did all of our usual Thursday things. I remember feeling proud, because Kali really seemed to enjoy it all. She laughed right along with Grandma Bernice and me as we decided how we'd like to die that week and who was going to be really sorry. But after that, things sort of went downhill.

Grandma Bernice and her quilting bee had just finished making my quilt the week before, so the next thing I did, after our usual Thursday stuff, was show Kali the new quilt on my bed.

"That's really pretty," Kali said when I took her upstairs.

"Yeah, and I helped make it," I bragged, even though I knew I was stretching the truth. The truth was that even though I'd gone to church and sat with Grandma Bernice and the other ladies in her quilting bee, no one ever let me so much as touch a needle. Mostly, they just let me help hold the quilt. So, basically, I'd been a holder. But when you're only eight years old, "holder" is the same as "helper."

"You're lying," Kali said. "You didn't help make that."

"I did too!" I said, hugely insulted.

"I'm going to ask your grandma," Kali threatened.

"Go ahead," I said.

Kali turned on her heel and headed for the stairs as I hurried after her.

"Grandma Bernice, Lula Bell says she helped make the quilt on her bed," Kali tattled.

"She sure did," Grandma said, smiling at Kali and giving me a quick wink as she ironed sheets in the living room.

Kali clapped her hands together, happy and excited all of a sudden. "I want to make a quilt, too! Can we do it now?"

Grandma's smile wilted just a little, like she was looking ahead and spotting some flashing signs: *WARNING! DANGER ZONE!* "Oh . . . well . . . not *now* . . . but maybe some other time," she tried.

Kali's face flushed. "That's not fair," she mumbled.

Grandma pretended not to have heard and continued ironing.

Kali stomped an angry foot at Grandma. "That's not fair!" she said again, louder. "It's not fair that *she* gets to make a quilt and *I* don't!"

The pleasant little smile dropped right off Grandma's face as she set the iron down on the ironing board. "Well now . . . it wouldn't be fair if Lula Bell was quilting while you were here and you weren't allowed to quilt right along with her. But nobody here is quilting."

"But it's not fair that she has a quilt and I don't!" Kali said in a shrieky voice.

Grandma's forehead bunched up like she was trying to think what to say. Finally, she came up with, "Don't you have some things at your house that Lula Bell doesn't have?"

For a minute, Kali just glared at Grandma. Then suddenly she said, sort of under her breath but loud enough for Grandma Bernice to hear, "I hate you."

Grandma's nostrils flared just a teensy little bit. "Do you even know what that word means?" she asked.

Kali lifted her chin, narrowed her eyes, and screamed, "Yes, and I HATE YOU, GRANDMA BERNICE!"

Grandma Bernice gasped. Then, she came thundering out from behind that ironing board like an angry bull let loose at the rodeo.

But Kali held her ground. She didn't move an inch. Not one inch.

When Grandma Bernice was standing right in front of Kali, she bent down, looked her in the eye, and quietly said, "We don't use the word 'hate' in this house. 'Hate' is a terrible word."

Kali just stared defiantly at Grandma, her face such a deep red that there were traces of purple.

"And anyway, you don't mean that," Grandma said.

"Yes, I do! I hate you! I hate you! I hate you!" Kali insisted with such fury that her body rocked back and forth with the words.

Grandma rose to every centimeter of her full height, stretching her back and neck upward and lifting her head high. Then, she looked down her nose at Kali and said, "I forgive you for saying that."

Kali didn't say a word.

Grandma continued, "But even so, you won't be setting foot inside this house again 'til you apologize."

Kali turned and headed for the front door, grumbling through clenched teeth, "I hate you. I hate your whole family!" Then she yanked the door open and slammed it shut behind her. The whole house shook.

Grandma's shoulders sagged. "Well now, she's certainly . . . *colorful*. I'd better go call her mama."

I still hadn't moved a muscle when Grandma came back from the kitchen.

"Lula Bell, you all right?" Grandma asked,

checking my forehead for fever with the palm of her hand.

I blinked at her. "Um, did you say you *forgive* her?" I asked then, because out of everything that had just happened, that was the part I found hardest to believe.

I couldn't understand it, and honestly, I was a little disappointed. I'd wanted Grandma Bernice to take a stand, to roar at Kali like a lion, and instead it seemed like she'd been a lamb, like she'd been weak when she should've been strong. I just couldn't believe it!

Grandma shook her head and said, "Honey, I feel sorry for her—I think somebody gave her the bears."

"Huh?" I said.

Grandma smiled as she dropped into her lazy-girl chair. "When you were about four years old, I took you grocery shopping with me. You wanted these little yogurt bears you'd seen on TV."

"Oh yeah, Yoge-Bears," I said, settling on the arm of the couch. "I remember those commercials."

Grandma nodded. "Well, those little plastic bears filled with yogurt were expensive so I refused to buy 'em. But I offered to buy you the exact same kind of yogurt in a regular cup."

"So I got the regular yogurt?"

"No, you flung yourself onto the dirty floor face down, flailing, crying, and kicking, right there in the refrigerated section."

"Oh my gosh! I'm sorry, Grandma."

She shrugged. "It's okay. It's okay now, and it was okay then. I knelt down, patted you on the back while you cried, and just waited for you to wear yourself out. Then we went home."

"That must've been embarrassing. I'm sorry," I said again. "I can't believe I did that."

"You only did it once," Grandma said, "because somebody took the time to teach you that throwing a hissy fit wouldn't get you what you wanted in life—everybody has to learn that at some point." Grandma stared at me like she was waiting for me to connect the dots.

It hit me like a bolt of lightning. "*Oh*," I said, looking at Grandma with wide eyes.

Slowly, Grandma nodded her head, and at the same time, we both said, "Somebody gave Kali the bears."

At school the next day, the day after Kali screamed at Grandma, Kali broadcasted to everyone at our lunch table what Thursdays were like at my house. It was the way Kali told it that made Grandma Bernice and me sound like freaks—like we wanted to die, like we couldn't wait to die, like we lived for death. Suddenly, my favorite thing about Thursdays—the obituary game—no longer seemed funny.

The day after that, on the way to school, Kali started making fun of me on the bus. By the end of the day, it seemed like everybody was talking about me, pointing at me, and laughing at me. Even kids who didn't know me. The more kids laughed at me, the more Kali tried to make them laugh at me—louder and longer, always wanting more—so of course, she began making fun of me on the bus on the way home, too. Within a week, everybody at school seemed to agree that I was a total freak—even my friends.

It's not like I never had friends. I had a few until Kali started picking on me all the time. But after that, everybody sort of kept their distance. Kids pretended not to hear me or see me. Nobody looked me in the eye anymore. All of a sudden, my former friends seemed very . . . busy.

Why? I don't know for sure—nobody's ever explained. Maybe my friends believed the things Kali said about me, or maybe they just liked Kali better. Whatever the reason, after a while, I just stopped trying. Trying felt too pathetic, like chasing after a bus you know you'll never catch. So I learned to move around the other kids instead of with them, like the moon orbiting the earth. I was part of their world but not really—not most of the time, anyway.

In fourth grade, when Emilou Meriweather's best friend had moved away near the end of the school year, we'd started a friendship—I thought. We waited for each other during our bathroom break, ate lunch together, and sat together under the big sugar maple during recess. But Kali hadn't been in our class last year. This year, when Emilou found herself in the same class with both Kali *and* me . . . well, what I saw most often was Emilou's back as she hurried away from me.

A few of the other freaks and geeks tried to reel me in: Fred Farber once sat beside me at lunch, but he smelled so bad that my eyes watered the whole time, and I tried to discourage him from doing it again. Another time, Gretchen Wells talked to me all through recess, but her voice was so high and so nasal that after a while, it gave me a headache. And then there was Alan West.

The truth is I didn't want to be one of them; I wanted to be one of the regular kids with regular friends. I *was* a regular kid with a regular voice, and I didn't stink at all! (Here's a little tip for you: if you are a borderline freak or geek and you start hanging around with the other freaks and geeks, I'm pretty sure that you aren't borderline anymore. I'm pretty sure that your freakdom—or geekdom—has been confirmed.)

Well, anyway, Kali never talked to me again after that day in third grade. Oh sure, she talked *at* me and *about* me plenty, but she didn't really talk *to* me, if you know what I mean.

Walking home, I tried to convince myself that school would be out for the summer soon and none of this would matter one bit—not Kali making fun of me, not the kids laughing, not the talent show. Only, I couldn't quite believe it.

Think of something else, I told myself as I looked around, searching for some kind of distraction. The hot-pink azaleas caught my eye, then the pansies standing in little groups, holding their faces up to the sun. But then I thought, *Even the pansies have friends.*

As I turned onto my street, the wind kicked up, and cherry blossoms floated around me like little pink feathers. I hadn't even noticed that the cherry trees lining both sides of my street had bloomed. And the blossoms were almost gone now. People come from miles around to drive down Cherry Tree Lane when it's in bloom, and I lived right here, walked by these trees every day, and somehow didn't even see them.

As I continued to look around, it seemed like everything had changed overnight: shades of brown and gray had given way to bright greens and reds and pinks and purples and yellows. The rocky, cold scent of winter had been replaced by a smell that was clean and sweet. Life hummed softly all around me—insects and birds and squirrels—where before there had been silence. This almost made me feel better, hopeful-like.

But then I saw my house, remembered that Mama would be there waiting, and knew that as soon as I walked in the door, she'd want to hear all about my audition. This thought was like a swift kick in the stomach. So then my stomach—*and my knee*—hurt. Ugh!

What a Mess!

I was relieved to find Mama on the phone when I walked into the kitchen, because that meant she couldn't ask me any questions—at least not right now. When she saw me, she held up her finger, as in, *One minute. Please wait.*

I nodded, noticing that our kitchen was a total wreck. There were three bags of groceries on the counter by the back door, waiting to be unpacked. In the kitchen sink, our breakfast dishes waited to be washed. On the other side of the sink was a cutting board, where potatoes waited to be cut. Near the stove sat a package of hamburger that had been defrosted in the microwave—I knew that because the edges had cooked and turned brown while defrosting—Mama hates that. On the other side of the stove, near the phone, the counter was loaded with stacks of bills and papers, Mama's checkbook, and stamps. On the table was a half-full laundry basket next to a folded stack of clean clothes. Next to the table stood the ironing board, with the iron sitting on top of it, sizzling and spitting.

I looked at Mama. She didn't look much better than our kitchen. She still had silver hair clips attached to her shirt, which was half tucked in and half hanging out. There were three pencils sticking out of her wild, messy hair—and Mama's hair was *never* messy. She looked tired, I decided—not mad-tired but tired-tired.

I felt tired, too. I slipped out of my backpack and let it fall to the floor.

Mama turned at the sound, still holding the phone to her ear. Creases appeared between her eyebrows as she looked from my backpack to me and back to my backpack again.

I couldn't believe that Mama thought my backpack was the problem here. It was as if she'd pointed out a single piece of trash as the problem at the city dump. *How did our kitchen get like this?* I wondered.

It couldn't have been Mama's fault. Mama is neat and organized. She likes for everything to have a place and for everything to be put in its place, not just left lying around. That's why we have things like the shoe basket, the glove basket, the mail basket, the key basket, the loose change basket, the remote control basket, the catalog basket, and lots of other baskets. We don't have a backpack basket though, so I picked up my backpack and carried it upstairs to my room.

When I came back down, Mama was off the phone. "Sometimes the other girls down at the shop just drive me crazy—I mean *really* crazy, like I'd like to rip out big fistfuls of my own hair, you know?"

Now I would've thought Mama was talking to someone else, had there been anyone else in the room. But since there wasn't, I said, "Yes, ma'am," as though I completely understood how the other girls down at the beauty shop might make a person barking mad, and I resisted the urge to ask, *Is that what happened to your hair?*

Mama looked at me as if to say, *Where did you come from?* But what she actually said was, "I thought you were going to call when you wanted me to pick you up."

"Um . . . well . . . it's such a pretty day, and . . . um . . . I thought . . . well, I just *wanted* to walk." I stopped talking because it wasn't exactly going well and shrugged my shoulders.

"How'd your audition go?" Mama asked.

"Um . . . fine," I lied. "Hey, did you see the cherry blossoms?"

"What?"

"The cherry trees—when they bloomed, did you see them?"

"I'm sure I did," Mama said in a way that told me she hadn't really seen them any more than I had. "Listen, Lula Bell, you're going to have to learn to iron. I'll teach you, okay?"

I couldn't believe I was being given extra chores now, on top of everything else—I hadn't even complained or anything!

The phone rang again, just as the dryer buzzer sounded, letting us know that another load of clean clothes was ready for folding—and ironing. Mama picked up the phone and motioned for me to sit down at the kitchen table, where she'd set out a box of cookies.

I sat down without touching them. Grandma Bernice had always said, "Cookies aren't supposed to come out of a *box*; they're supposed to come out of the *oven!*"

Mama scurried after her papers, her beauty supply catalogs, and her calendar, all of which were littered with yellow Post-it notes. Meanwhile, I tried to push the whopping lie I'd just told about auditions out of my head, along with Kali Keele—and the ironing that awaited me.

I wished Daddy were home. He knew all about auditions and might've understood—and been able to explain it to Mama. If not . . . well, at the very least, Daddy should've been here for ironing lessons—because most of the time he wore clothes that looked like he'd slept in them.

Who's the Omega Wolf Now?

The first thing I learned at school on Thursday morning was that a few of the kids in my math class hadn't done their homework, which was long, long, *long* division—not hard but still time-consuming. Anyhow, they didn't have their homework, but they did have a plan. By the time math rolled around, they'd convinced everyone in our class to pretend that Mrs. Sharp hadn't given us any homework, that she'd forgotten to assign it or something.

So late that morning, when Mrs. Sharp said, "Get out your homework," nobody did.

Instead, we all looked around at each other like, *Huh?*

"What homework?" someone said.

"You didn't give us any homework, Mrs. Sharp," someone else said in a very helpful-like voice.

Mrs. Sharp looked like she was trying to think back to yesterday. "Yes I did. I *know* I did," she said.

"Nuh-uh," Zeke Baxter argued weakly. He'd probably done his homework, I thought—Zeke always did his homework.

Mrs. Sharp put her hands on her hips and looked around the classroom. When she locked eyes with Alan West, she shook her head and sighed a sad sigh. "I'm going to have to give all of you zeros on last night's assignment."

Alan swallowed hard, but he didn't say anything. That is, he didn't say anything until Mrs. Sharp picked up her grade book. Then, Alan's hand shot up in the air.

"Yes, Alan?" Mrs. Sharp said like she had no idea what he was going to say. She knew what Alan was going to say all right—we all did.

Alan said, "This isn't going to go on my *permanent record*, is it?"

"Well . . .," Mrs. Sharp said. Then she hesitated

and bit her lip, like she sure hated to give Alan West a zero on his permanent record.

"Because I plan to go to Harvard University. I've been planning it my whole life—'Harvard' was the first word I ever said," Alan informed her.

Mrs. Sharp sighed. "Harvard has awfully high standards, and there's a lot of competition. It'll be tough to get in there, Alan . . . especially if—"

Before she could even finish, Mrs. Sharp had Alan West's homework from the previous night in her hands. So everyone in our class—except for Alan, who'd gotten extra credit, too—got a zero on the previous night's homework. When Mrs. Sharp had finished writing big, fat zeros in her grade book, she got up from her desk.

"I'm very disappointed in all of you," she said quietly. Then she added, "Some more than others." And she looked directly at me!

Grandma Bernice would've been disappointed in me, too, I knew. But that's just because she never understood about trying to fit in. She said so herself. Whenever I'd tried to talk to her about fitting in, Grandma had always said, "I just don't understand why you want to *fit in* when you're made to *stand out*." Then she always broke out singing, "This little light of mine, I'm gonna let it shine . . ."

For a minute I thought about getting up to turn in my homework. I glanced over at Alan. His eyes were already on me, desperate and urging. But I looked away, stayed in my seat, and left my homework where it was—folded inside my math book.

It was a good thing I did, too, because everybody was really mad at Alan. I was mad at him, too, but either he didn't notice or he didn't think it was *that* big a deal.

At lunchtime, as usual, Alan got in line behind me and followed me all through the cafeteria to the same table where he sat across from me every day.

"So," Alan started.

"Could you please not talk to me, *please*," I interrupted.

Alan glanced down at his mound of spaghetti and shrugged. "Okay, but why? Do you need to study?"

I rolled my eyes. "No, Alan. Only you would ever think to use lunch as a study period." I hadn't meant for it to come out sounding as mean as it did.

"Right," he said.

I looked around, lowered my voice, and said, "I'm sorry. It's just that I'm trying to fit in and make some friends, and you . . . you . . . aren't helping."

"Sure, of course, yes, I understand," Alan said too quickly. His cheeks reddened so that the white, circular scar on his left cheek stood out; his neck was also turning red, as the angry rashy thing that always appears when Alan is upset began to bubble up; he scratched at it.

DEFCON two, I thought, moving over one seat to put some space between us so that it wouldn't look like Alan and I were together. And do you know what? It worked! At least that's what I thought when Emilou Meriweather stopped alongside my table on her way to dump her lunch tray.

"Hey, Lula Bell," Emilou said, casting a quick glance behind her before she continued. "What'd you get on your social studies test?"

I'd gotten an A—I get mostly A's—and I opened my mouth to tell Emilou so but closed it again. Something told me this wasn't the right answer, the regular answer, the *fitting in* answer.

"Ummm, a C?" I guessed, hoping this was the right answer. *Has to be*, I told myself, because C is average, right? "What'd you get?"

"I got a B," Emilou said, wincing, like she really hated to tell me.

Why? Why would—oooh, she feels sorry for me because I got a C, I realized then. *B! I should've said B!*

Emilou tossed her wavy red hair, glancing back over her shoulder again. Then she leaned down and said quietly, "I just wanted to tell you that I planned to invite you to my birthday party . . . only Kali said I couldn't."

I didn't know the right answer to that either: Thanks? Okay? Whatever? Fitting in was hard work, I decided.

Emilou straightened up and looked around the cafeteria nervously. Kali was coming with her tray, but before she could spot Emilou with me, Emilou was gone.

I shouldn't have complained that Alan wasn't *helping* me, I realized later, because for the rest of the day, he tried to do just that. Now, granted, Alan didn't talk to me, because I'd told him not to. But still, he loaned me a pencil when I couldn't find mine, rushed to pick up my library book when I dropped it, and grabbed my arm to keep me upright when I tripped over my own two feet during gym class. That was when I'd had enough.

I yanked my arm away from Alan and yelled, "Stop it! Stop it right now! JUST LEAVE ME ALONE, ALAN!"

Sneakers squeaked against the gym floor, skidding to a stop. Everyone looked. First they looked at me, then they looked at Alan, and finally they looked at each other as if to say, *Uh oh, she's losing it! She's losing it, man!*

Alan showed me his palms as he backed away from me. For a split second, he looked so hurt, I thought he might cry. It passed so quickly, though, that afterward, I wasn't even sure I'd seen it— maybe I'd just imagined it. But I *did* see Alan's face turn red and big splotches erupt on his neck as he lowered his head and nodded at his feet. And I wondered, *Who's the omega wolf now?*

Temporary Insanity

When I finally climbed onto the bus that afternoon, relief washed over me. Another day was almost done. I'd almost made it. I plopped down on a seat in the middle of the bus, alone, and put my backpack next to me so that Alan couldn't sit there. Then, I rested my head against the window and closed my eyes.

As kids poured into the bus, it filled with chatter and noise, but still, I kept my eyes closed. When someone behind me bumped my seat hard, I kept my eyes closed. When the doors clattered closed and the bus began moving, I kept my eyes closed.

I kept my eyes closed right up until I felt something hit my shoulder. I looked up just in time to see a brown, wadded-up lunch bag bounce off me onto the floor. It reminded me of the brown paper bag Grandma Bernice had brought to school for me when I'd forgotten my lunch at home. It reminded me of how I'd skittered right past Grandma in the hallway, like maybe I didn't even know her, when she was so happy to see me.

I thought about how happy I would be to see Grandma Bernice now, anywhere, anytime, how I would run to her and throw my arms around her. If only I could have one more chance. I leaned my head back and blinked at the metal ceiling, trying to make the tears in my eyes go back to where ever they came from.

Just then, I heard Kali Keele call out from behind me, "What's the matter, Lula Bell? You look like you lost your best friend. Awww, that's right. You did! You lost your *only* friend! Your grandma's finally gone, isn't she? Well, I'm glad, because—"

"Kali!" someone gasped.

And then silence.

Suddenly I was fully alert and shaking with so much hurt and regret, anger and outrage that I thought I might explode.

"*I'm* her friend," Alan said from the seat across the aisle, loud enough so that everyone on the bus could hear him.

I didn't need or want his help. Hadn't I made that clear?

"Shut up, geek! No one's talking to you!" Kali snapped.

I turned around in my seat. "*You* shut up, Kali! Nobody here is interested—nobody here even *likes* you! They're just scared of you, that's all."

Kali held on to the back of the seat in front of her and stood up to look down on me. "*What* did you just say?" she asked.

But of all the things I felt, none was fear, so I said louder, stronger, and with more certainty than I'd ever felt in my life, "I *said* people don't *like* you! They're just *scared* of you because you're so mean!"

The bus was silent. No one so much as moved a muscle.

Ashton Harris, the girl sitting beside Kali on the bus, stared at me with terrified eyes, and I knew that what I'd said was right. Ashton was scared of Kali, and she was even more scared now that her secret was out.

The bus jerked to a halt, hissing, and the doors

squeaked open. I looked around and recognized my stop. Calmly, I gathered up my stuff, climbed down off the bus, and started walking home, never looking back.

In our yard, Grandma's pink tulips and yellow daffodils shifted slightly with the breeze. They seemed to be waving me in, like cheerful little fans waiting at the finish line. *Thanks, girls*, I thought.

I zipped up the front walk, let myself into the house, and shut the door behind me. I wiggled out of my backpack and dropped it on the floor. Then, I hurried to the front window to get a look at Alan and Kali as they passed by. Alan lagged far behind Kali, shifting his eyes back and forth between Kali and my house. Meanwhile, Kali trudged on, occasionally swatting at her face. She looked like she might be crying.

Good! I thought. Only I didn't feel good. My stomach felt sick, and I still wanted to scream—or cry—or both. What I didn't want to do was talk—to Mama. Besides, I'd reached my feeling-sorry-for-myself limit with her.

"Lula Bell? Is that you?" Mama called from somewhere upstairs.

I stepped back from the window and hollered,

"It's me! I'm going outside to ride my bike!"

"Good!" Mama hollered back. "Be home before supper!"

With that, I ran for the garage. I grabbed my bike, hopped on, and pedaled down the street, away from my house, as fast as my legs would take me.

Rules Are Made to Be Broken—Right?

I wasn't planning to go there. Honest, I wasn't. When I left the house, my only thought had been, *Away*. And when I reached the stop sign at the end of our subdivision, all I knew was that I had to keep going. Now, I am not allowed to ride my bike outside of our neighborhood. I knew this, had always known this, had never once broken the rule. Until now. I didn't even know why I was breaking the rule; all I knew was that something inside me said, *Keep going*. So I did.

When I arrived at the cemetery, I figured as long as I was there, I might as well say hello. I got off my bike and parked it in the grass by the big, scrolly, black iron gate. Then I tiptoed around, careful not to step on anybody, until I found her.

The flowers were gone, but Grandma Bernice's headstone had been put in place. It was smooth and shiny and read "Bernice Francine Bell." Below her name were the dates of Grandma's birth and death, just like she'd wanted, and below that it said, "She left the world a nicer place."

For a minute, I thought Grandma's headstone was missing the word *for*, as in, "She left the world *for* a nicer place." But then I remembered how many times had Grandma Bernice said, "Always leave a place nicer than you found it," and I understood.

I stretched out on the grass beside Grandma and laced my hands together behind my head. I wished that we were both stretched out on her bed at home, talking and giggling like we used to do, but then I closed my eyes against the blazing late-afternoon sun and pushed forward the way I had all week.

After a little while, I began talking. I told Grandma Bernice everything that had happened since she'd died. I even told her what had happened on the bus that day. Grandma didn't answer me. I hadn't really expected her to—I probably would've jumped out of my skin if she had. But I had expected to feel better in some way, and the fact is, I didn't. I just felt lonely and even sorrier for myself.

The insides of my eyelids turned from red to black. I opened one eye a slit.

Mr. Jimmy, the gravedigger, was standing over me, blocking out the sun. "She ain't here," he said.

"You've already told me that," I informed him. "And honestly, it'd be a lot more helpful if you could tell me where Grandma Bernice *is* instead of where she *isn't*."

"Don't know," Mr. Jimmy said. Then he stepped aside, causing the sun to practically blind me. I squeezed my eyes shut.

After a few minutes, I blinked and sat up. I didn't see Mr. Jimmy anywhere. I stood and dusted off my backside.

"Well . . . um . . . bye, Grandma," I said to the polished rock with her name on it. Then I looked around, hoping nobody had heard me.

That's when I decided Mr. Jimmy was right: Grandma Bernice wasn't here. But where was she, then? How could I know, really know, that she was anywhere? What if she wasn't? What if Grandma Bernice wasn't there, wasn't in heaven—what if there wasn't any heaven? What if Grandma Bernice was just gone, really gone, forever? These questions piled up, one on top of another, on top of me, all the way home, until they were almost more than I could bear.

I pedaled faster and faster, as if I could somehow escape them if only I went fast enough. I held onto the handlebars so hard my hands hurt, and I pedaled with all my might. But I still wasn't fast enough.

I stopped pedaling and coasted. The cool breeze should have been soothing, but it wasn't. It wasn't soothing at all.

The Trouble with Death, Curly Q Shampoo, and Fitted Sheets

Our kitchen was clean—or at least clean*er*—when I got home. The only remaining mess was made by the cleaning products themselves, still sitting on the counter: powders and sprays and brushes and sponges. A mop stuck out from one side of the sink, while the other side held a bucket full of dirty water.

"Supper's almost ready," Mama said. "Go wash up."

Mama's hair was up that day, but pieces of it had fallen down around her face, and she'd left them right where they fell. Also, even though I'd ironed it, Mama's blouse was a little wrinkly, but she seemed too busy to know or care, and I surely wasn't going to point it out.

When I came back from washing up, what I noticed wasn't the two perfect place settings Mama had put out for us but the empty spot where Grandma Bernice's place setting should've been. It was as if death had torn through our kitchen like a meteorite, leaving a giant hole in our table, our lives, our hearts. And now, three and a half weeks later, Mama was trying to pretend it had never happened, like the holes weren't there. I didn't think I could do it. I didn't think I could stand to sit there that night, facing the great, gaping hole that Grandma Bernice had once filled.

"Aw, Mama, can't we just eat in front of the TV like everybody else?" I tried. "Daddy's back out on the road again, Grandma Bernice is . . . *gone* . . . it's just the two of us anyway—and we could watch the Animal Channel." (Mama likes the Animal Channel, too.)

Mama turned from the stove. "No, Lula Bell. I've planned a nice supper, and we're going to sit down at the table and eat it, just like always."

"Do we have to?"

Mama set her wooden spoon down and came

over to me. She took my shoulders in her hands. "Yes, we have to do things like we would normally do them. That's the only way I know. If we *act* normal, then maybe in time we'll start to *feel* normal."

"Okay," I immediately agreed, because I was relieved that Mama was prepared. She had a plan. I didn't, and at that moment, I figured any plan was better than no plan.

Even so, our supper table seemed unbearably quiet and empty, just as it had every night that week. No one laughed. No one broke into song or brought up reincarnation or flapped their hands like wings. No one fought to get a word in edgewise. In fact, no one had anything to say. Instead, Mama and I just sat there looking at one another and trying not to mention the great, gaping hole, even though I'm pretty sure it was all we could think about. I know it was all *I* could think about.

"How was your day?" Mama tried.

"Fine," I lied.

"Good," Mama said.

For a few minutes, there was only the sound of forks and knives on plates. Acting normal was turning out to be much harder than I thought—it was almost as hard at home as it was at school.

"Oh!" Mama said, like she was relieved to have come up with something to say.

I looked up hopefully.

"Mrs. West is expecting you tonight at 7:30. She says you're doing great, by the way. She says you're almost ready."

I forced myself to swallow the baby peas in my mouth and said, "Ma'am?"

"Surely you haven't forgotten—Lula Bell, the talent show's only a couple of weeks away now!"

Right. The talent show. The talent show I was supposed to be in but wasn't. At that moment, I figured I had two choices: 1) Tell Mama the truth, or 2) Show up at Alan West's house right after supper. Since neither of those choices was tempting, I searched my brain for a third option. Maybe if I practiced the three *p*'s—if I was practical, well prepared, and punctual, leaving at just the right time (during good weather)—I could run away from home. I thought about that for a minute but wasn't excited by the idea of living in a tent or under a bridge—I'm more of an indoor girl. So, I went through my options again: *Should I tell Mama the truth?*

"Lula Bell?" Mama said.

"Oh, yeah . . . 7:30, okay," I said, because this, a mere meal, was hard enough as it was. The truth surely wasn't going to help.

After supper, Mama put me to work in the living room, ironing sheets. They didn't smell the way they used to when Grandma Bernice had washed our sheets, because she always hung them outside instead of putting them in the dryer. But even so, I was grateful I only had sheets to iron that day— because sheets don't have collars, sleeves, folds, or buttons, all of which cause me big ironing problems. I breezed through the pillowcases and flat sheet, all the while singing a song Daddy's band played:

Some folks don't like our laundry
hangin' out there on the line,
oh, but they don't know
what it's like to wear sunshine
Down here . . .

That's when the trouble started, because I was left with the fitted sheet, which had elastic that pulled and pushed and fought me every step of the way. Still, I did okay—until I tried to fold it. The fitted sheet wouldn't fold into a neat little square like the other pieces because of that darn elastic! I tried and tried, but as soon as I'd get one side right, the other side loosened and became an uneven mess. I went from frustrated to furious. Letting out a low growl, I kicked that sheet as hard as I could. The sheer force of this kick somehow yanked my other leg out from under me, causing me to sail through the air and hit the ground like a sack of potatoes.

Mama must've heard the boom, because she peeked in from the kitchen, finding me on the floor. "What happened?"

I shrugged. "I had a fight with the fitted sheet."

"And the sheet won?"

"Fitted sheets are unpredictable—and dangerous," I informed her. "They really should be outlawed."

I was in no mood to play or sing or even hear any music during my music lesson—and I certainly didn't feel like going on with the show—so I hesitated. But just like always, Mrs. West insisted, "The show must go on!" So it did, and once I got going, the music swept me up and carried me away. I forgot about everything else, including time.

Mrs. West must've forgotten about that, too,

because when she glanced down at her watch, she gasped. "Oh my stars! I had no idea how late it was getting—your mama's probably worried sick!"

"That's okay," I said. "I'll just call her. Can I use your phone?"

"I don't know—*can* you?" Alan said, laughing from his perch at the top of the stairs. "Do you know how to use a telephone?" He seemed to think he'd just told a terrific joke. (Here's a little tip for you: grammar jokes aren't that funny.)

I rolled my eyes. "*May* I use the phone?" I said to Mrs. West, correcting myself.

I got a busy signal.

It was so late by the time I got home that there was no one waiting for me—or so I thought until I climbed the stairs.

"Lula Bell?" Mama called from her bedroom.

I pushed her door open a little more and said, "Ma'am?"

Mama was putting the phone back, and I knew then that she'd been talking to Daddy. I wished I could've talked to Daddy, too.

"I was waiting for you," Mama said. "I . . . I thought you might like to sleep with me in the big bed tonight."

"Really?" I said.

Mama smiled. "Really. Go put on your pajamas, brush your teeth, and come back."

I nodded. When I returned, Mama was watching the Animal Channel on TV. As I climbed into the big bed with her, the new Curly Q Shampoo commercial was just starting. "Look! Look at that!" I said. "You just wash your hair, and *bam*! Curls."

Mama smiled. "It looks that way on TV, but that's not how it works. It doesn't *make* curls. It's just a shampoo for people who already have curly hair."

"Are you sure?" I asked.

"I'm sure," Mama said. "I use Curly Q at the salon sometimes. It helps prevent frizz, that's all."

"How is that right?" I asked in a shrieky voice. "The Curly Q people shouldn't be allowed to get people's hopes up like that!" (Look, some of us want to go to Harvard while others merely want curls. Is that so much to ask?)

Mama turned off the TV. I tried to calm myself with slow, deep breaths. Mama's room smelled like a mixture of fabric softener and hair products—clean and fruity.

As we lay there together in the dark, Mama said,

"I'm thinking of selling the beauty shop."

I forgot all about the evil Curly Q people then. "How come?" I asked.

"I don't know . . . I don't think it makes me happy anymore."

"But you love to do hair, Mama."

"I know I do. It's just that doing hair and running a business are two very different things and—well, anyway, I'm only thinking about it."

"Okay," I said.

For a while I just lay there, listening to Mama's breathing grow deep and even. "Mama?" I whispered, not sure if she was still awake.

"Hmmm?"

"I thought you said we have to do everything like we always did, like normal." *This isn't normal,* I was thinking.

Mama sighed. "I know, and I do think that. I think we have to go on with school and work and lessons and meals the best we can."

I listened.

"But," Mama continued, "I guess we have to be flexible, too. We have to adjust some, to be there for one another, to help one another when it's really hard."

I understood. Nights were hard for me, too. There was too much quiet, too much time to think, to wonder, to question, to doubt.

Mama reached over and patted my leg, rescuing me from my own thoughts.

Faith is the substance of things hoped for, I remembered.

"This is nice," I said then, because it was.

May the Force Be With You

By Friday morning, I had come to my senses, and knew I'd made a big mistake: Kali Keele was going to make me pay for what I'd said to her on the bus the day before. For a few minutes, I thought about trying to get out of going to school, but then I realized that wouldn't solve my problem. If Kali didn't get me that day, she'd get me whenever I showed up at school. *Might as well get it over with,* I thought, since I probably wouldn't be allowed to quit school.

As I parted my hair in the bathroom mirror, I wondered if Kali might go so far as hitting me. By the time I left the house, I'd decided it would be best to tell Mama that any injuries were the result of a fall or some sort of accident. Because the last thing I wanted was for Mama to call the school or Kali's parents (or worse, show up in person) and make a big fuss—which would only make things harder for me.

Since it was drizzling outside, Mama hollered to me on my way out the door, "And for the hundredth time, bring your raincoat and boots home!"

"Yes, ma'am, I will—I'm sorry," I hollered back and shut the door—quick—behind me.

When I got down to the bus stop, I found Alan standing as straight and as stiff as the stop sign next to him, holding a black umbrella in one hand and his briefcase in the other—he looked like a professional fifth-grader, I thought. Meanwhile, on the other side of the stop sign, Kali stood hunched over, head down, hood up, so that I could barely make out her face. Neither of them looked at me.

Might as well get it over with, I thought again and gave a little cough to announce my arrival.

Nothing. *Huh.*

By midmorning, I realized that my Friday was turning out much better than I'd expected. I felt myself relax just a little. And then I made a big mistake: I smiled at Alan West.

I didn't mean to. It was kind of a reflex. I was sitting at my desk, doing my work, and when I happened to look up from my paper, I locked eyes with Alan. So I smiled at him, just a teensy little bit, just so it wouldn't be awkward.

And this was enough. It was enough to encourage Alan, apparently, because at lunchtime, he made his way over to the seat across from mine, nodded at it, and said, "May I?"

I looked behind me. There were only three kids left standing in the cafeteria, waiting to pay. Everybody else had already gotten their food and chosen a seat. Nobody had chosen to sit with me. I shrugged.

Alan pulled the chair out from under the table and sat down. He didn't talk much, at least not to me. But Alan looked like he might've been having a back and forth conversation with himself in his mind. He made different faces and seemed to be working up to something. He checked the clock. Occasionally, he sort of nodded at me. I sort of nodded back. We exchanged a few reflex smiles. But mostly, we just ate our lunch.

Emilou Meriweather stopped alongside my table, on her way to dump her tray. I smiled up at her.

Emilou didn't smile back. "I heard about what you said to Kali yesterday," she said.

I looked across the table at Alan, like, *Uh-oh.*

Alan scratched at his neck.

"Kali shouldn't have said anything about your grandma," Emilou continued. "I . . . I . . . well, I just don't know what I'd do if she ever said anything about *my* grandma—we're very close."

I nodded my understanding.

"May the force be with you," Alan said to his lunch tray. I knew this was Alan's *Star Wars* way of wishing Emilou good luck with Kali.

Emilou looked at me, as if to say, *Well, that was weird!*

I tried to give her a look back that said, *I know!*

Emilou forced an uncertain smile and said, "Okay . . . well . . . bye," and hurried away.

As soon as she was gone, Alan checked the clock again, then sat up straight and cleared his throat. "Lula Bell, I memorized a poem for you."

"Huh?" I said.

Alan nodded. "It's believed to have been written by Mary Elizabeth Frye. It goes:

Do not stand at my grave and weep,
I am not there; I do not sleep.
I am a thousand winds that blow,
I am the diamond glints on snow,
I am—"

I laughed. I laughed so hard that I nearly fell out of my chair. I couldn't help it. At first I was confused by Alan's outburst of poetry. After that I was a little uncomfortable—poetry isn't exactly normal lunch-room behavior. Then, I felt nervous and embarrassed, and a giggle bubbled up inside me. I tried to let it out through my toes by wiggling, but it didn't work. It was like trying to let the Atlantic Ocean out through the kitchen faucet. The giggles just kept building inside me until I had to clap a hand over my mouth to keep them inside. But one escaped through my nose. It was all downhill after that. Once I got started, I couldn't stop laughing. It was like being in church—knowing I wasn't supposed to laugh only made it worse.

I was still laughing but trying to stop when Alan stood, picked up his tray, and left the table.

When music class was almost over, our teacher, Miss Arnett, said, "Lula Bell, I'd like to have a word with you after class, if you don't mind."

I stayed in my seat after the bell rang, my toes wriggling in my shoes, while the rest of my class filed out, into the hallway.

When the room was empty, I stood and went to Miss Arnett's desk. "Ma'am?" I said.

"I'm afraid I need a favor," Miss Arnett said.

I nodded for her to go ahead.

"Ginny Olmstead has sprained her ankle and won't be able to perform her dance in the talent show."

"I'm sorry to hear that," I said.

"I'm sure Ginny would appreciate that," Miss Arnett said. "At any rate, I need another performer to fill her slot."

"Oh," I said. "Okay . . . well . . . I'll try to think of someone."

Miss Arnett smiled. "How about you?"

Me? "But I didn't even audition," I said. "Maybe I don't even have a talent."

"Everyone has a talent," Miss Arnett said, "and I've heard a lot about yours. We *really* need you."

"You do?"

Miss Arnett laughed a musical little laugh. "Just think it over and let me know by the end of the day."

"Okay," I said.

When I was almost to the door, Miss Arnett said, "Lula Bell?"

I turned around. "Ma'am?"

"I want you to know that I'd consider it a personal favor to me if you decided to do it."

I really liked Miss Arnett. She was young and pretty and smiled easily. I really wanted to do her a favor. But still, I'd have to think about it.

It turned out to be a no-brainer. If I performed in the talent show, Mama would never have to know how I'd chickened out at auditions and then *lied* to her about it—repeatedly. Plus, I'd get to do Miss Arnett a favor.

I stopped by the music room that afternoon, on my way to catch the bus. I poked my head in the door and found Miss Arnett stacking the blue folders that were filled with sheet music.

"Okay," I said.

Miss Arnett turned and smiled when she saw me. "Okay, I'll do it."

"Wonderful!" Miss Arnett said. "Come to the gym on Thursday, right after school, for dress rehearsal."

By the time I got off the bus on Friday afternoon, I'd decided I owed Celia Thompson big time. Since Celia had worn her fiery rain boots that day, I figured Kali and her friends must've been so busy talking about those boots that they forgot me— mostly. Because what else could've kept Kali from giving me grief that day? I sure hoped "the force" was with Celia—and Emilou. Hey! Maybe "the force" was with *me*!

Hmph!

When the doorbell rang late Friday afternoon, Mama looked at me and said, "I hope it's not another creamy onion and green bean casserole."

"Me, too," I said, crinkling my nose. (Here's a little tip for you: nobody wants any kind of vegetable casserole when someone has died—or ever, if you ask me. When you're hurting, you don't want to be healthy; you want to be comforted. Brussels sprouts and green beans are not comforting. Macaroni and cheese, mashed potatoes, fried chicken with gravy, homemade potato chips and ice cream—now *those* are comfort foods!)

I followed Mama to the front door, where we found Mrs. Purdy from Grandma Bernice's quilting bee.

"I hope you weren't in the middle of dinner," Mrs. Purdy said as she stepped inside.

"Not at all. Please, come in, sit down," Mama said. "Would you like some iced tea?"

"No, thank you. I can't stay. I just came by to drop this off," Mrs. Purdy said, handing Mama a big shopping bag.

I eyed the bag suspiciously and listened for the sounds of Tupperware. Now, I'd always liked Mrs. Purdy, but I wasn't sure I'd be able to forgive her if she'd brought us a whole shopping bag full of creamy onion and green bean casseroles. But no, I'd *have* to forgive her, no matter what was in the bag, I decided, as soon as I remembered the Purdys' annual Fourth of July picnic. I couldn't risk missing that party.

The Purdys have fainting goats on their farm. Fainting goats are goats that faint dead away whenever they're scared. One minute they're standing there, looking at you with their goat eyes, and the next minute they're lying on the ground with their eyes rolled back in their heads. And that's not even the best part. The best part is watching the people—grown-ups!—as they try to scare those poor goats into passing out every Fourth of July. I think Mr. Purdy likes that part, too, because he stands by his goats and says stuff like, "Nope, they've seen that before. Try again."

Mama looked puzzled, but she accepted the shopping bag and said, "Thank you."

Hey, would a baby fainting goat fit into a shopping bag? I wondered, just for a split-second.

Mrs. Purdy touched the pearls at her neck and said sadly, "It's the last quilt Bernice ever worked on . . . and we all thought you should have it."

Okay, so it wasn't a baby fainting goat, but it wasn't a green bean casserole, either. Usually, Grandma's quilting bee gave their quilts to sick children who were in the hospital for long periods of time, to make their hospital rooms and beds feel homier and comfier. But occasionally, they made quilts for their own families or for people from our church who were going through hard times.

"Thank you," Mama said again, but softer now and with more meaning.

Mrs. Purdy hugged her. "I'm praying for you, precious."

When Mrs. Purdy was gone, Mama lowered herself onto the couch and said, "Just give me a minute, Lula Bell."

I nodded, knowing that Mama was trying to keep it together, trying not to cry. When I heard soft whimpering sounds, I busied myself with looking inside the shopping bag. I didn't think I should leave Mama alone when she was upset like this, but I didn't think I should stare at her either—staring is never polite.

I pulled the edge of the quilt out of the bag and gasped.

Mama's head snapped up.

I spread the quilt out on the living room carpet. We both stared.

When I'd finally taken it all in, I had to bite the insides of my cheeks to keep from laughing. The quilt was one humongous neon rainbow. In the center was a pastel striped unicorn with a monstrous metallic gold horn jutting out of its forehead. The result looked like something that had been plucked out of a deeply disturbed, completely crazy mind.

Now Grandma Bernice had made some of the most beautiful quilts I'd ever seen, but this quilt, well . . . "hideous" is the word that springs to mind. But no, let's just say that I am not a rainbows-and-unicorns kind of girl and leave it at that. Mama is not a rainbows-and-unicorns kind of girl either. Apparently.

Mama's eyes widened and her mouth dropped open as she looked over the quilt. For a minute, she didn't say anything. Then, she burst out laughing.

I was so relieved, I laughed, too.

Mama laughed so hard that tears continued to pour down her face. She rolled back and forth on the couch. It was contagious. Neither of us could stop. We laughed until we could barely breathe.

Finally, Mama sat up. She took deep breaths, trying to calm herself. Then she smiled. "Those are Grandma's fabric remnants—*all* of them."

I looked back at the quilt again and exploded in another fit of laughter.

"I'd been after her to get rid of those remnants for forever, telling her how she'd never find a use for all of them, so she . . . she . . . she"—Mama squealed with laughter—"she found a way to prove me wrong—it's not a very pretty way, but it's a way just the same."

I could almost hear Grandma Bernice saying, "Hmph!"

"What in the world will we ever do with *that*?"

"Hide it in the linen closet?" I suggested, which started Mama laughing again.

"We have plenty of quilts already," I finally said.

"Agreed," Mama said.

"So maybe we should give this one away."

Mama looked at the quilt again and said, "A person would have to be homeless and freezing to death to accept this. We'll have to wait 'til winter."

We laughed some more.

That night, as Mama tucked me into bed, I said, "Maybe we should keep the quilt, just to remember and to make us laugh," because it felt so good to laugh again and to hear Mama laugh again, too.

"That quilt is the most unforgettable quilt I've ever laid eyes on," Mama said, her hand resting on my light switch. "I say give it to anybody who'll take it, *please*." And with that, she turned the light out. I could hear her laughing all the way down the hall.

The Betrayal

Monday was the kind of May day that made me want to stay home from school and go crawdad fishing in Honey Run Creek. The sun was shining, and there were no signs that it would stop—only the faintest little wisp of a cloud streaking across the blue sky. But then I remembered that Grandma Bernice was the only one in our house who knew how to clean and cook crawdads.

And anyway, nobody in my class stayed home that day. The entire fifth grade showed up to go on the field trip to Confederate hero Sam Davis's plantation in Smyrna, Tennessee, about an hour away by bus.

Of course, Alan West and I were bus buddies, pretending the poetry incident had never happened. But as soon as I stepped off the bus onto the gravel, Emilou Meriweather called out, "Lula Bell! Lula Bell!" Then she motioned for me to come with her.

My heart jumped for joy. Quickly, I turned and handed Alan his *Star Wars* lunchbox. "Well . . . have fun!" I said cheerfully. "I'll see you later."

Alan raised one eyebrow, giving me a kind of parental look, as if to say, *I'm very disappointed in you, young lady.* (I know that look well, because I've gotten it from Mama a lot.)

I rolled my eyes at Alan and started to walk away.

"Lula Bell," he said, sounding desperate as he took a step toward me.

I stopped and faced him.

Alan took a deep breath and seemed to steady himself.

"*What?*" I demanded. Couldn't he see that I was in a hurry?

"Have you noticed that I'm your friend *all the time?*"

I shrugged. "I guess."

"And have you noticed that you're only *my* friend when it's convenient for you?"

"What're you trying to say?" I demanded.

Alan looked like he really, *really* didn't want to answer me, but finally, he did: "I'm saying that either you're my friend or you're not . . . all the time."

"Okay, then I guess I'm not," I said as quickly as I could, because I really had to go—Emilou was waiting.

As Emilou and I followed the rest of our class toward Sam Davis's home, I glanced back at Alan. He was standing right where I'd left him, beet red from his forehead to his collarbone, clutching his lunchbox with one hand and feverishly scratching his neck with the other. *DEFCON two*, I thought, and for a few seconds I wondered what happened when Alan reached DEFCON one. Did he scream? Cry? Explode? Just fall over like a fainting goat? Honestly, I was glad I didn't know.

Emilou and I stuck together as the class went inside, toured the big white house, and listened to a lecture on life during the Civil War, which was given by women wearing big, round hoopskirts.

We stuck together outside as we walked the same dirt paths that had been used for more than a hundred and fifty years—the dirt even smelled old—and I saw some of the biggest trees I've ever seen in my life. We stuck together as we crammed into the cottage that sat on the edge of Stewart's Creek (called the Creek House) for a lecture on Civil War medicine—or lack of it—during which I held on to my chair with both hands and tried not to vomit, while Emilou rested her head face down on the table in front of us, using her arms to cover her ears. I have two words for you: cannon balls. Need I say more?

If you ask me, it's a miracle that any Americans survived the Civil War, and I'm not even talking about the war or the medical practices, which were too grim and grisly to even go into here. I'm just talking about basic hygiene. For example, after doing their business, soldiers wiped their behinds with a corn husk, the same corn husk they carried around in a little bag with their plates, cups, and toothbrushes! Honestly, it's easy to see how germs claimed more lives than weapons, don't you think?

After the medical lecture, we went back to the big house and were ushered into a small movie theater-style room, where we watched a film about Sam Davis. I figured Sam Davis was probably a hero for killing lots of enemy soldiers, but it turns out, he was a hero because of the way he died. Man, Grandma Bernice would've loved him!

In 1863, Sam Davis was captured by Union soldiers and charged with being a spy for the Confederacy, which he was. Then, Sam was held prisoner and told repeatedly by Union forces that his life would be spared if only he would give up the names of other Confederate spies. If he didn't, he would be hanged. Sam was only a few years older than I am, and he must've been terrified. Still, he wouldn't give up a single name. Instead, he'd proclaimed, "If I had a thousand lives, I would give them all rather than betray a friend." True to their word, the Union hanged Sam Davis, and true to his word, Sam Davis gave his life rather than turning his back on his friends. Even his executioner had cried, which I could understand—I felt like crying for Sam, too.

After the movie, we gathered out in front of Sam Davis's home.

"Everyone find a spot on the porch—and stay on the porch," Mrs. Pritchett commanded, her hands cupped around her mouth. "It's time to eat lunch."

The wooden planks under my feet shook as kids took off running in a race for the best spots on the wraparound porch. Emilou shuffled her feet and seemed to be waiting for me. I couldn't have been happier or prouder if I'd had a peanut butter and grape jelly sandwich with the crusts cut off—which, incidentally, I did.

"Over here!" Kali called, waving her arms. "Come sit with us!"

By "us," Kali meant Ashton Harris, Hannah Green, Rebecca Lynn Rayburn—all the girls who'd laughed at me. I looked at Emilou, uncertain.

"C'mon," she said as she walked toward Kali. I followed.

Just as Emilou and I were about to sit down, Kali stared at me and sneered, "Not *you*, Lula Bell! You can't sit with us!" Then she laughed her mean laugh and said, "You know, Emilou, if you want to adopt a stray, that's fine. But the rest of us . . . we don't bring our *pets* to lunch."

I could feel my face turning red. "That's okay," I said quickly to Emilou before I turned and walked away. I left the shade of the covered porch behind and sat down in the sun, on the porch steps, about as far away as I could get from Kali and her crew without actually leaving the porch.

I felt sick, too sick to eat. And I felt lonely. Kali

was right. I was like a stray dog—no pack, no people, no place to belong. I was a lone wolf. I remembered the omega wolf then and tried to tell myself that it was better to be a lone wolf than an omega wolf, but honestly, neither seemed like much fun.

I looked around for Alan, thinking I'd find him with Richard and Bill, but I didn't. I finally spotted Alan in a lone rocking chair, outside the gift shop, eating his sandwich and reading the paperback book I'd seen in his back pocket that morning. He looked perfectly content. He and his book were doing just fine.

I wished I were fine. I wished I could get up and go sit with Alan. I wished I could talk to him. But what would I say? I guessed I could—and should—apologize, but I hate apologizing. So I stayed where I was and unpacked my lunch. I figured that would at least make me *look* fine. But I didn't eat a bite.

By the time we got back on the bus, I still didn't know what to say. Alan must not have known what to say either, because even though we sat together—we were still assigned bus buddies—we never said a word to each other. It was a long ride back to school.

I thought about Grandma Bernice and the way

she had always said, "That Alan West is a smart boy, and handsome, too!" *Smart, yes,* I thought, *but handsome?* I turned and snuck a look at Alan as he read his book. I didn't see handsome. All I saw was hair—and a splotchy, scratched-up neck.

Then, I remembered the last time I'd complained about Alan to Grandma Bernice. It was last October, because Alan had been busy carving a pumpkin during my music lesson. "When he walked me to the door, Alan told me I smelled nice," I'd told Grandma, making a disgusted face.

Grandma Bernice had smiled. "That Alan West, he's a smart boy, and handsome, too!"

"I don't think you understand," I said. "He was *sniffing* me! I mean . . . *ew.*"

Grandma seemed to think about this. Then she crossed her arms over her chest and said, "I knew a boy like Alan when I was in school."

"You did?" I said, pulling out my chair and joining her at the kitchen table. "Tell me."

Grandma's eyes rolled up toward her forehead and stayed there as she tried to remember. "Well, back in grade school, there was this boy who was really smart, but he was going through sort of an awkward stage. It was just his age, you know."

I nodded.

Grandma continued, "Anyway, this boy liked my friend, Florence, so when Valentine's Day came around, he brought a big, fancy box of chocolate to school and gave it to her."

"What happened?" I said.

"As soon as he walked away, Florence threw the box of chocolates in the trash, but the boy turned back just in time to see her do it. And he never forgot it."

"How do you know?" I asked.

"I know because later, in high school, this boy became very tall and muscular and handsome—he was a real hunk!—and then Florence wanted him to take her out on a date. Finally, *she* asked *him* to take her out, which no girl did in those days, and he refused. He took me out instead."

I leaned forward. "Was Florence mad?"

"Oh yes, but mostly she was mad at herself." Grandma giggled. "And I'm sure Florence got over it . . . when that boy and I got married."

My mouth fell open.

Grandma Bernice nodded. "His name was Roy, and he was your grandfather."

It was almost as hard for me to imagine my

granddad as "a hunk" as it was to imagine Alan as one. But I kept trying.

Again, I turned and looked at Alan and tried to see past any awkward stage. He might grow taller. He might get muscles, although I doubted it. But let's face it: there are no awkward stages for hair. You get what you get and it is what it is for your entire life. For Alan, that meant a lifetime of disastrous hair. For me, it meant a lifetime without curls. I sighed.

After that, I thought about Sam Davis for a while. I tried to put myself in his shoes: would I be able to give up my life to save my friends? What friends do I even have who would be worth saving? Since I didn't have any friends, I figured I'd get to live. *So good!* I thought. *Except . . .*

"I'm your friend all the time," I remembered Alan saying. And when I really thought about it, he was right. Alan had chosen me every chance he'd gotten. He'd sat with me at lunch whenever I would let him. He'd sat with me on the bus, even though he knew that Kali Keele would probably make fun of me there—and he'd tried to help me with that. He'd even stood up for me on the bus in his own way, claiming to be my friend when Kali said I didn't have any friends. He'd loaned me pencils. He'd tried to keep me upright when I tripped over my own two feet. He'd brought me flowers after Grandma Bernice had died. He'd lugged a huge stack of books and assignments home for me when I'd been absent—which couldn't have been easy, since he had his own stuff to carry, too. And, I suspected, he'd told Miss Arnett that she ought to put me in the talent show—who else could it have been? He'd even memorized poetry for me.

And still, somehow I hadn't ever really considered Alan until now. Somehow, I hadn't *really* seen him in the same way that I hadn't really seen the cherry trees bloom.

No, in return, I'd ignored Alan, asked him not to talk to me, yelled at him to leave me alone, laughed at him, and ditched him every chance I'd gotten, including that morning. And then I'd told him I wasn't his friend. And it was true. I'd never really been Alan's friend, not the way that he'd been mine, not in any way that really mattered. I felt sick again. Only this time, I was sick with shame.

Emergency! Emergency!

Over the next few days, I came to dread all freedom at school, times when other kids got to relax and enjoy hanging out or playing with their friends: waiting for the bus, riding on the bus, gym class, recess, and especially lunch. I dreaded this freedom because I had no friends, no hope of having friends, and never was this fact clearer to me—or more embarrassing—than during those times.

I wished we had assigned seats all the time, even at lunch, even on the bus. I wished no one was ever allowed to have any fun at all, because then it wouldn't seem so weird and awful that I wasn't having any.

Anyhow, without any friends or fun to slow me down, I was the first one, except for Miss Arnett, to arrive in the gym after school on Thursday.

Miss Arnett smiled and came right over when she saw me. "Oh, Lula Bell, good," she said, like I was the person she'd most hoped to see that afternoon. "Do you have a costume you need to change into?"

"Um, no, ma'am," I said. *Do I need a costume?* I wondered.

"Perfect," Miss Arnett said. "Then why don't you go ahead and do your number for me while the other kids are still arriving and getting changed." It wasn't really a question.

"Um . . . okay," I said, even though I'd been counting on a little more time to warm up to the idea of performing.

Miss Arnett smiled and nodded encouragingly as I climbed the steps, sat down at the old upright piano, and placed my sheet music. Then I looked down at her. She was writing something on her clipboard as a few girls trickled in to the gym and headed for the girls' locker room.

Miss Arnett looked up at me and said, "Whenever you're ready."

I just sat there, wiggling my toes. A few more kids

arrived in the gym and headed for the locker rooms.

After a couple of minutes, Miss Arnett said, "Did you forget something, Lula Bell?"

I shook my head.

Miss Arnett clipped her pen to her clipboard, folded her hands in her lap, and waited.

I placed my fingers on the piano keys and found that they knew exactly where to go and what to do. "Under the Boardwalk" flowed right out through my fingertips—it was even easy! Well, it *was* easy, 'til it was time for me to start singing.

Then, all of a sudden, my mouth dried up like it was full of sand, and tidal waves began crashing through my stomach. I broke into a sweat, and my head felt light. I thought I might throw up or pass out—or both. All I could do was play the song's intro again and again, buying extra time.

But the longer this went on, the sicker I got. I did what I think anybody else would've done under the circumstances: I jumped up off that bench and sprinted to the girls' bathroom. And it was a good thing I did. I just barely made it to the toilet in time!

I was wiping my mouth with the scratchy brown paper that passes for paper towels at our school when Miss Arnett came into the bathroom to check on me.

"Lula Bell, sugar, are you sick?" Miss Arnett said.

Sick? Yes! That's it! I'm not scared; I'm sick! I nodded my head and tried to look puny, which wasn't exactly hard.

"Do you want me to call your mother for you?"

"No, ma'am," I said, doing my best to sound really pitiful. "I think I can do it myself."

Mama was busy at the salon, so I left a message for her, telling her that I was sick and she should come get me. Then I waited outside. I couldn't risk Mama running into Miss Arnett.

It seemed like I was out there waiting for a long time. I began to worry that dress rehearsal would end before Mama arrived. If that happened, I'd have to hide behind the garbage Dumpster to keep Miss Arnett from noticing me and waiting with me for Mama—which I wasn't exactly looking forward to since I could already smell the garbage from where I was.

And what if it started raining? The sky was a solid blah-gray, as if somebody had taken their old string mop into the paint store and asked that the sky be painted exactly the same color. So rain wasn't out of the question.

Just then, I spotted Mama's car careening around the corner. When it jerked to a stop in front of me, I noticed that Mama looked a little . . . mad. How could she be mad at me? She hadn't even talked to Miss Arnett!

It all was too much: the loneliness, the fear, the sickness, the waiting and worrying, and on top of it, Mama was mad at me. I started crying as soon as I was in the car with the door shut.

Mama's face softened. "Are you all right?"

I shook my head. "Where've you been?"

"I'm sorry," Mama said. "I came as soon as I could."

"Grandma Bernice would've come right away," I wailed.

"I know. But Grandma Bernice didn't have a business to run. There was a hair emergency at the salon."

"A *hair* emergency?" I repeated, just so Mama could hear how ridiculous that sounded—hair wasn't an emergency; vomiting was an emergency!

"Yes, my new stylist, Teresa, had some trouble coloring a client's hair."

That hardly sounded like an emergency to me. I mean, how much trouble could Teresa really have had? Had someone's head erupted in flames? Had someone lost an eye? Had there been bloodshed?

"Blond can be tricky," Mama tried to explain. "If you don't leave the color on long enough, the hair turns orange, and if you leave it on too long, it turns white."

This still didn't sound like an emergency to me, and I didn't want to ask, but for some reason, I really wanted to know: "What color was Teresa's client's hair?"

Mama smiled a little, remembering. "White. Solid white, like Grandma Bernice's hair."

I stuck my chin out and said, "Well, *I* always thought Grandma Bernice's hair was pretty."

"It was," Mama said easily, "but Teresa's client couldn't have been older than twenty-five."

"Oh," I said, still thinking about Grandma Bernice's curly white hair. "Hey, maybe you could give me a perm."

"Perms are even trickier than color. Do you know what happens if you leave a perm on too long?"

"No, ma'am." I wiped my face on my sleeve and waited for her to tell me.

"When you rinse the perm out, the hair is stretchy while it's wet."

Now I admit that stretchy hair sounded pretty bad, but still, I said, "I *really* want curly hair."

Mama continued, "And after that, when the hair dries, it turns brittle, breaks, and falls off. All of it."

Okay, so maybe I didn't want a perm after all.

"You're not running a fever," Mama said after she felt my forehead. In Mama's book, you have to run a fever to qualify as sick.

"I know," I mumbled, wishing with all my heart that I did have a fever so that Mama would put me on the couch, cover me with a quilt, fix me homemade chicken noodle soup, and make me feel better somehow.

Uh-Oh

What with my emergency and all, I'd forgotten that Daddy would be home, but I was sure glad to see him. He didn't seem so glad to see us though. When we came through the door, Daddy was sitting at the kitchen table with a gigantic piece of chocolate cake in front of him. When he saw us, his face dropped and he froze, his fork midair.

"John Bonner!" Mama gasped. "You are *not* about to spoil the supper I've planned and shopped and prepped for, and am about to cook, by eating half a cake!"

Daddy put the fork down. "You just missed Claira Reese—she brought the cake."

Mama huffed and headed for the stairs.

Poopoopahduke! I thought. *If only I'd been here a teensy bit earlier, and if only Mama had been here a teensy bit later!* (Here's a little tip for you: if you drop off any kind of junk food or sweets at a house where the mama isn't home but the daddy or the children are, the mama will probably never know you came by.)

"Oh yeah," Daddy hollered after Mama, leaning sideways in his chair, "and Claira said to be sure and tell you she's praying for you."

"You should've asked her to pray for *you*," Mama hollered back.

"What? I was just going to *taste* it," Daddy muttered to himself. Then he grinned at me.

We moved Daddy's cake onto a paper plate and ate it over the trash can so we could drop the whole thing the second we heard the stairs creak, the second we heard Mama coming. It was good cake. When we were finished, Daddy poured us both a glass of milk while I rushed to rinse our forks and get them in the dishwasher, getting rid of the evidence.

"Are you ever scared when you're onstage?" I asked.

"Always. I'm *always* scared at first," Daddy said, handing me my milk.

"Then why do you do it?" I said.

Daddy leaned back against the counter while he thought about it. "It's what I'm meant to do," he finally said. "And once I get past the fear, I know that. I can feel it. I know I'm right where I'm supposed to be."

"How long does it take you to get past the fear?"

"Just a few minutes—a few minutes, every night," Daddy said.

I felt a little sorry for Daddy then. If his fear was anything like my fear had been that day . . . well, I just couldn't imagine going through that almost every night of my life.

"You know, Lula Bell, being brave doesn't mean *not* being afraid," Daddy said. "Being brave and having courage mean going ahead even though you are afraid."

"You must be really brave, Daddy."

"I must be," Daddy said, chuckling.

Mama came back into the kitchen then, having changed her clothes. "I have to get supper started," she announced, which was a nice way of saying, *Get out of my way,* to Daddy and me.

I got out of her way immediately, noticing that Mama didn't exactly sound happy about starting supper.

Daddy must've noticed, too, because he said, "Aw, c'mon now, you're not still mad about the cake, are you?"

Mama shook her head as she washed her hands. "You have no idea what I'm going through, John. You just . . . you have *no idea*."

Daddy crossed one foot over the other and settled into leaning against the counter. "Then tell me," he said. (He should've gotten out of Mama's way. That's what I thought.)

Mama finished drying her hands and threw the towel on the counter in an angry, frustrated gesture.

Uh-oh, I thought.

And I was right. Boy, did Mama ever tell Daddy.

"Okay," Mama said. "I hit the ground running every morning, John. I rush to get myself ready, get Lula Bell up and ready, feed her breakfast, see her off, clean up, plan and start supper, and get myself to work. By the time I make it to work, I feel like I've already run a marathon, but my day's just starting, and I have to continue running, working as fast as I can, to get everything done, so that I can leave and be here when Lula Bell gets home from school. But I never get everything done, so I have to spend the rest of my afternoon trying to put out fires over the phone and on the computer. Meanwhile, I'm trying to be a decent mother and cook and housekeeper—do you know that I've started choosing my clothes based on what color the next load of wash is going to be?"

Daddy shook his head.

"Well, I have," Mama said. "And I've started keeping a cooler in my trunk, just in case I'm able to leave the salon long enough to get the grocery shopping done, which never happens. Whatever I do, it's not enough. I'm always behind, always frantic, always frazzled, and always wishing my mother was here to help me. Which makes me miss her even more, and . . . and . . ."

Daddy pushed off from the counter and took a step toward Mama, like he was going to give her a big hug.

But Mama pointed her finger at him and said, "And *you*! All you have to do is take care of yourself—dress yourself, feed yourself, make it to the show on time. You only have *one* job, while I'm here juggling *ten*!"

"Is that my fault?" Daddy said quietly.

Mama thought about this. "No," she admitted just before her face crumpled and she started crying.

Daddy did hug Mama then. Which only seemed to make things worse. Mama cried so hard that it sort of scared me. I'd never seen her come apart like this.

"I just miss her. I miss her *so much*," Mama sobbed into Daddy's shoulder. "It's not fair that she's gone—it's just not fair—she never would've wanted this for us, for *me* . . . she . . . she . . ."

"Grandma Bernice got what she wanted for *herself*," I said then. "She even died the way she wanted—"

"Not now, Lula Bell," Daddy interrupted.

I closed my mouth.

When Mama was all cried out, she let go of Daddy and took a step back. Her whole face was blotchy and wet, and little straggly pieces of hair stuck to it in odd places and formations. She left it that way.

"Everything's going to be okay," Daddy said. "You'll see. We'll work it all out somehow."

"But how?" Mama said.

"I don't know yet," Daddy admitted. "But I know we'll figure it out."

"John, I'm just so tired. I've never been so tired in all my life."

"Go and rest then," Daddy said. "I'll fix supper."

Mama rested, and Daddy fixed the only supper he knows how to fix: he picked up the phone and ordered a pizza.

That night, after I took a bath, Mama called me into her bedroom.

"Sit down," she said, pulling the stool out from under her dressing table for me.

I did as I was told.

Mama parted my wet hair and combed it. Then, without saying a word, she started sectioning my hair and wrapping it around pink sponge rollers.

"Curls! Curls! You're giving me curls!" I exclaimed.

"I'm trying," Mama said. "That's all I can do."

"Thank you!"

For a few minutes we were quiet as Mama continued rolling my hair. I loved watching her work in the mirror. She was so neat and orderly. She had a rhythm: section, comb, roll, clasp; section, comb, roll, clasp.

"I have to tell you something," Mama said then. Section, comb, roll, clasp.

"Okay."

"It's not good news," Mama warned. Roll, clasp. I waited.

"Uncle Cleburne's sick. He's in the hospital," Mama said. Her hands went still.

I turned around to face her. "Is he going to die?"

"I don't know, Lula Bell. He's very sick," she said quietly, lowering her head.

"Oh, Mama, what should we do?"

Mama lifted her head and looked at me. Her eyes were sad. "Cousin Ethel wants me to come...tomorrow."

I nodded. "You should take some sweet tea. Great Uncle Cleburne loves your sweet tea. I bet that'll perk him right up."

"But, Lula Bell," Mama said, "you're performing in the talent show at school tomorrow."

Oh yeah, that. I thought for a few minutes. Finally, I said, "Um, I don't really think that's going to work out . . . but I *do* know that Great Uncle Cleburne and Cousin Ethel need you."

"It's all going to work out beautifully, you'll see," Mama said.

I shook my head. "It's scary up there on that stage, Mama. I wish somebody could be up there with me, you know?"

"I bet Grandma Bernice'll be with you in spirit."

"Yeah . . . I meant somebody wearing *skin*."

Mama laughed her breathy little laugh. She just didn't understand how scared I really was.

"There," Mama said as she clasped the last roller in my hair.

"Thank you," I said.

Mama knelt in front of me and placed a hand on my knee. "Lula Bell, I can see that you're scared, but I know you can do this. You'll be fine, just fine. You'll see."

Maybe I will, I thought. *Maybe I can do it, since my hair's going to be curly and all.*

"And Daddy'll be there," Mama promised.

My stomach turned over. What would he think if I froze up onstage—or worse?

By the time I closed my eyes that night to try and sleep, which wasn't easy with the rollers in my hair—rollers curl your hair by *pulling* it, apparently—I'd decided that if I couldn't perform in the talent show, I'd distract Daddy by breaking out my Second Place Science Fair ribbon. I figured that between my ribbon and my curls—especially my curls!—he couldn't be too terribly disappointed in me. Could he?

It All Began with Curls

On Friday morning, for the first time in my life, I was sorry I'd stuffed my raincoat into the lost and found box. It was raining, and I had curls to protect—curls!—not to mention I was wearing a Sunday dress. As a result, I had to wear Grandma Bernice's raincoat, which was covered in huge polka dots of all different colors—I'm pretty sure we could've spread it out on the floor and played Twister on top of it. This was far worse than wearing my own raincoat—obviously. Even so, I didn't dare take it anywhere near the lost and found box. Instead, when I arrived at school, I went directly to the music room without even bothering to take off the coat.

"Do you still want me to be in the talent show?" I asked Miss Arnett as I stood in front of her desk, dripping.

Miss Arnett looked a little surprised. I didn't know if it was me or my Twister raincoat or the rain running off me, forming little puddles on her floor. Or maybe it was my curls.

But then Miss Arnett smiled. "Yes, of course, if you're feeling better."

I nodded and felt the curls in my hair move back and forth. "Okay then," I said, and I turned to leave.

"Your hair looks pretty," Miss Arnett called after me.

The talent show started right after lunch, which worried me, because my stomach was then fully loaded. But when I found out that I'd be the last person performing, after twenty-two other acts, I calmed down a little. *Plenty of time*, I told myself. *Time for my food to digest a little, time for me to calm down a little, plenty of time.*

I stood off to the side of the stage, just behind the blue velvet curtain, wearing the red dress that

Grandma Bernice had loved best on me. Once, I peeked out from behind the curtain, but when I saw what had to be nearly every student in the entire school, plus teachers and some parents, too, well . . . I decided not to look out there again—it wasn't exactly calming or helpful to the digestive process. So I focused all my attention on what was happening on the stage.

Miss Arnett stood in front of a microphone, thanked everyone for coming, and talked about how the money from ticket sales would help the music department. Then she introduced the first act. It was a juggling act set to music. Nobody else backstage paid any attention, but I thought Mike Tate's juggling was pretty good. I liked it.

I liked most of the acts, even Kali's. Although I hated to admit it, Kali and her friends were pretty good dancers. They weren't *great* dancers, but they were good, unified, and peppy—like dancing cheerleaders. Plus, their song was bouncy and happy.

But my hands-down, absolute favorite number was Celia Thompson's tap-dancing act. First of all, Celia had on a bright purple costume covered in sequins. Second, she danced to "I Feel Good," which made *me* feel good. Third, Celia Thompson is a terrific tap dancer—you should've seen her! She made great, wide circles around the stage with her feet moving and tapping so fast, you could barely keep your eyes on them. It was like she was a drummer, only she tapped out rhythms with her feet. By the time Celia was done, I wanted to rush right out and sign up for tap-dancing lessons. Only I couldn't, because it turned out that I was the next act in the talent show. When I heard Miss Arnett say my name, my stomach flipped.

I took a deep breath, reached up and touched my curls—just to make sure they were still there— and walked out onto the stage.

Miss Arnett looked mighty relieved.

I took my place at the piano and unfolded my "Under the Boardwalk" sheet music. Then I adjusted the microphone and spoke into it.

"This is for the best friend I ever had," I said.

Just then, a spotlight hit me. At least, I thought it was a spotlight. But when I looked, I realized that a single beam of sunlight had broken through the rain clouds and was streaming in through a window in the back of the gym. It landed right on me, just like a spotlight!

I could hear people murmuring to one another

in the audience, but I ignored them and placed my hands on the piano keys. I closed my eyes and began playing. But what came out wasn't "Under the Boardwalk."

My eyes flew open in panic. I didn't know what to do, so I just kept playing. I played the intro twice while I tried to figure it out. I knew I couldn't just stop and say, "Ooops!" into the microphone—just imagine what Kali could do with that juicy little tidbit. "Ooops!" would become her new favorite word.

So, I did the only thing I could think to do. I went with it. After all, I knew the song; it was one of the first songs I'd ever learned. I settled, closed my eyes again, opened my mouth, and sang:

This little light of mine, I'm gonna let it shine!

Oooh, this little light of mine, I'm gonna let it shine!

This little light of mine, I'm gonna let it shine!

Let it shine! Let it shine! Let it shiiine!

That's about where I was when the audience started clapping along with the song. It gave me courage. I opened my eyes as the piano and my voice grew bigger and louder and stronger. I was right where I was supposed to be, doing what I was made to do—I could feel it, just like Daddy had said. I felt like a bird that had leapt out of the nest, expecting to hit the ground with a sickening thud, only instead, I'd discovered I had wings. I was soaring, I tell you! *Soaring!*

As the last note rang out through the gym, my spotlight went dark. Chills climbed up the back of my neck. And then the audience was on its feet, clapping and cheering and whistling.

When I stepped off the stage, Celia Thompson was waiting behind the velvet curtain, bouncing up and down on her tap shoes. "That was *awesome!*" she said.

I felt so grateful, I threw my arms around her. Celia hugged back, and we both bounced. *I really need some tap shoes,* I thought.

When we stopped hugging, I stepped back and said, "I loved your number! It was my favorite! I gotta learn to tap dance! Where do you take lessons?"

"At Barbara Ann's," Celia said. "But . . . if you want, you could come over to my house some time and I could show you."

"Really?"

Celia nodded and smiled a shy smile, "And maybe you could teach me some about singing."

Just then, I spotted Mr. Jimmy, the gravedigger, above the crowd. He was coming toward us.

Mr. Jimmy leaned down and kissed Celia on the cheek. "Good job," he said.

"Thanks, Daddy," Celia said. "This is Lula Bell—could she come over some time?"

Mr. Jimmy nodded his head and smiled. "Your grandma was your best friend, hunh?"

I nodded and waited for Mr. Jimmy to say something like, *Well, she ain't here.* But instead, Mr. Jimmy said, "She was here. Right here. Today."

For a few seconds, I thought about that. He was right. I had felt it. I had felt *her.*

Then I spotted Alan. He was hanging back, behind Mr. Jimmy and Celia, looking down at his feet, his face so flushed that his scar stood out like a white neon sign against his skin. He seemed to be nervous—*really* nervous. And he seemed to be waiting.

"Alan! Alan!" I said, waving him over.

He looked around and pointed to himself like, *Who, me?* Then slowly, he walked toward us.

When he was close enough, I looped my arm through Alan's and said, "This is my friend, Alan West."

Celia said, "I know you! You're really smart! You're going to Harvard!"

Mr. Jimmy looked impressed.

"Hi," Alan said to both of them in an *Aw shucks* kind of way.

"Oh, gosh, what happened to your face?" Celia said, staring at the circular scar.

I froze. Only my eyeballs continued moving around while Mr. Jimmy and Celia waited for an answer.

Alan looked confused and said nothing. Then he touched the old scar on his cheek, like he'd forgotten it was there, and said, "Oh. My cousin Joel Caleb and I were playing *Star Wars* in the backyard."

"Uh-huh," Celia encouraged.

Alan continued, "But we didn't have light sabers, so we used sticks instead."

Celia nodded.

"We were playing like our sticks were swords— you know, like they do in the movie," Alan said.

"I love that part," I said.

Alan smiled a half-smile at me and nodded. "Me, too. Anyway, Joel Caleb accidentally put his stick through my cheek."

"Wow," Celia said, as if Darth Vader himself had

made the scar on Alan's cheek. "What did you do?"

"Well," Alan said, "there was a lot of blood coming from my face, and it frightened me. The human body only holds about ten pints of blood and can expire from a loss as small as twenty-five percent. So I tried to run to the house to get my parents."

"Expire?" Celia said.

"Tried?" I said.

"*Expire* is a nice way of saying *die*," Alan said. "And yes, I tried to run for the house, but Joel Caleb tackled me and sat on top of me, and he's older and bigger than I am."

"Omigosh! Why? Why would he do that?" Celia said, her voice rising an octave.

"Corporal punishment," Alan said. "Joel Caleb kept saying, 'No, Alan! No! Please! My mama's going to whip me good for this!'"

Celia leaned toward Alan with wide eyes. "So what did you do?"

"I screamed until my parents came outside. Joel Caleb tried to put his hand over my mouth, but I bit him," Alan said. "Did you know that human bites are the nastiest, worst bites one can suffer?"

Mr. Jimmy, Celia, and I were quiet for a few seconds, taking all of this in.

Then I said, "So what happened to Joel Caleb?"

"Oh," Alan said, "his mama whipped him good."

We all laughed—especially Mr. Jimmy—and then Alan did, too.

When we stopped laughing, Alan turned to me and said, "You look pretty, Lula Bell. I like your hair."

I folded my thumb over my palm, held up my hand, and opened my mouth to ask Alan how many fingers he saw. But before I could, he smiled and said, "Four."

I nodded. "Thanks."

"I like your hair, too," Celia said. "I've always loved your hair. It's so shiny, like the hair you see on shampoo commercials."

"Really?" I said.

Celia nodded enthusiastically.

"Thanks," I said. "I've always loved your flaming rain boots."

For a few minutes, we all just stood there, smiling at each other, feeling happy and . . . *full* somehow.

Then the principal's voice came over the intercom: "All students whose families *aren't* here should return to their classrooms immediately."

"Oh! My daddy!" I said. "I have to find him!"

Celia gave me a little wave as she walked away, and said, "I'll see you soon, Lula Bell—tap-dancing at my house!"

I faced Alan, nervous all of a sudden. For a second I thought about just turning my back and walking away. *No*, I told myself. *Ask! Ask now!*

My toes were wiggling like mad as I cleared my throat. "Um, could you wait right here, Alan, just for a minute or two? I really need to talk to you." Then I waited for Alan to say something like, *I will never, as long as I live, wait for you, or walk with you, or sit with you, Lula Bell Bonner!* I figured Alan had every right, and I owed it to him to stand right there and take it.

But Alan's whole face lit up. "Sure!" he said so quickly and so eagerly that it almost broke my heart in two.

"Thanks," I said. "Be right back."

"I'll wait as long as I can," Alan called after me. "My parents aren't here, so I might be sent back to class, but I'll wait as long as I can. Right here. I'll be right here."

I turned and nodded at him as he craned his neck, trying to keep me in his sight.

People kept stopping me on my way to find Daddy, telling me how much they loved my song. Most of them commented on the beam of sunlight, too. Some people seemed to think I'd had something to do with the light, like my act was one part singing, one part piano playing, and one part magic trick.

Ginny Olmstead came up to me and said, "It was worth spraining my ankle to see *that*. How do you do it?"

"I don't . . . I didn't," I said. "It was just the sun."

Ginny looked confused. "What was? I'm talking about your song."

I thanked her. I thanked everyone.

Finally, I found Daddy, right outside the gym. He looked like maybe he'd been crying. *It's probably just allergies*, I told myself, and I really hoped that I was right this time.

Daddy put his arms around me and said, "That was *spectacular*! I thought you were going to blow the doors off the place!"

"Thank you," I said, relieved.

Emilou Meriweather spotted Daddy and me and rushed right over. "Oh, Lula Bell!" she said as she hugged me. "You did so good!"

"Thanks," I said as I stepped back.

Daddy draped his arm around my shoulders as we stood there side by side.

"You know," Emilou said to us, "I wanted to have a karaoke birthday party."

I shook my head, like, *No, I didn't know.*

"Uh-huh," Emilou said, "but Kali said that wasn't cool. Only now, I've decided to do it anyway. It's *my* birthday party, and I love to sing!"

"Ummm . . . that's great, Emilou," I said.

"Yeah, there's just one thing," Emilou said. "You have to promise that if I have a karaoke party, you'll come. You have to *promise.*"

I smiled. "I promise."

Daddy squeezed my shoulder. When Emilou was gone, he said, "Miss Arnett told me to tell you what a great job you did and to thank you."

I nodded.

"She said you were a regular hero, the way you stepped in to help her out with the talent show, at the last minute and all."

For a split second, I panicked. But then I remembered. "Hey, did you know I got second place in the school science fair?" I said.

Daddy shook his head. "Wow," he said. "A

musician *and* a scientist?"

That sounded pretty geeky, but still, I nodded and smiled, relieved.

Alan must've had to go back to class, because when I went back to the gym, looking for him, he was gone. Out of the corner of my eye, I spotted Kali Keele walking away on her way back to class, too. She was alone. I guessed her friends were with their parents, and then I wondered, *Where are hers?*

For the rest of the afternoon, all anyone at school talked about was my performance and the beam of sunlight that had turned on and off with perfect accuracy and timing. It seemed like I had a lot of friends all of a sudden, which was a nice feeling—a *new* feeling.

On the bus that afternoon, Ashton Harris and Brittany Cook argued over which one of them should get to sit next to me. Ashton won, apparently. When we reached my stop, I said good-bye to Ashton, climbed down the steps, and waited for Alan.

Kali was the next person off the bus, and I watched her as she walked past me like she didn't see me. Kali didn't exactly look upset or mad, I decided, but there was something there, something different, more like . . . loneliness? Unhappiness? Both?

"Grandma Bernice would've been proud of you today," Alan said as he came to stand beside me.

I didn't say anything, just started walking. I was still trying to think what to say to him.

"I know how you feel. I know you miss her," Alan said. "I still miss my grandfather, Big Dad. He died last year."

I sort of remembered something about Alan's grandfather dying but hadn't paid attention at the time. I tried to make up for it now. "What was Big Dad like?" I asked quietly.

Alan thought about it. "Gentle, patient, smart, *really* smart. Kind of nerdy, like me, I guess."

My eyes widened in surprise. Who would've guessed that Alan West *knew* he was a nerd? And if he knew . . . well, why didn't he stop? I wanted to ask but thought that might be rude. So, instead, I said, "I'm sorry, Alan. I was wrong."

"About what?" Alan said.

I thought about it and shook my head, not knowing where to even start. "Everything, I guess. I thought I needed friends, but I already had one, a true friend, a friend like Sam Davis."

Alan puffed up a little bit. "That's okay," he said. "I knew you'd come around . . . eventually. And I'm a very patient person."

I smiled. "You are. You really are. Just like Big Dad."

Alan smiled back.

By the time we got to my house, I had figured it out. Of course Alan West knew he was a nerd— he was smart! But being who he really was, all the time, was Alan's way of letting his light shine all the time.

Welcome to Bizarre-O-World

On Saturday morning, I carried Grandma Bernice's crazy rainbow-unicorn quilt downstairs and said to Daddy, "I'll be back in a little while."

"Uh . . ." Daddy seemed to be thinking. Eventually, he came up with, "Where're you goin'? When will you be back? What's the quilt for?"

I smiled. "You almost sound like Grandma Bernice."

Daddy sat up a little straighter. "Well?" he demanded, just like Grandma Bernice.

"I'm going to the spaceship house; I won't be long; and the quilt's a gift."

Daddy scratched at the stubble on his chin, thinking. "Where'd you get it?"

"Grandma Bernice made it," I said.

Daddy thought about this and then shook his head slowly. "I don't know. Your mama . . . *her* mama . . . well . . . I just . . . I just don't know about this."

"Mama knows about it," I said. "She told me I should give it to anybody who'll take it."

"Maybe I ought to call her," Daddy said, getting up.

"Go ahead," I said. "I'll wait."

Daddy watched me carefully. He seemed to be deciding something. "Naw," he decided, breaking into a grin as he sat back down. "If you say she told you to do it, I trust you. I don't reckon you like making your mama mad any more than I do."

"No, sir," I said.

"Then I'm sure you're doing the right thing."

I hoped I was doing the right thing, but I wasn't exactly sure.

The house was easy to find even though I'd never been there before. It was easy to find because it didn't really seem to fit in with the rest of the houses in the neighborhood. Mama called it "modern"; Daddy and I called it "the spaceship house."

I took a deep breath and knocked.

Kali Keele opened the door. When she saw me, her face hardened. "What do you want?" she said.

"Nothing," I said. "I just came to give you this."

Kali eyed the folded quilt in my arms as if it might be stuffed with spiders instead of batting. I held it out for her to take it.

But Kali didn't take it. Instead, she stepped back from the doorway and said in a clipped voice, "Come in."

Once I was inside, I couldn't imagine why on earth Kali wanted a quilt. A quilt seemed to be the exact opposite of just about everything in her house. It was all hard edges and clean, open spaces. There was lots of glass and stainless steel and no color at all—unless you count black, white, and gray as colors, which I don't. The result was a house that felt cold and lifeless. There wasn't even a houseplant in there.

Suddenly, I understood why Kali had wanted a quilt so badly. The girl *needed* a quilt in the worst way. In fact, as far as I could see, everybody in her family needed one. Quilts are colorful and soft and warm. They speak of life and love and family and home.

I closed my mouth. I hadn't known it was hanging open until then.

"So," Kali said, crossing her arms over her chest. "You're here to give me a quilt?"

"Yeah," I said.

"Why?" she demanded.

"Because you want one . . . or you used to."

That's when I realized Kali probably didn't even want a quilt anymore. Just because she'd wanted one in third grade didn't mean she wanted one now, when she was almost in sixth. When *I* was in third grade, I wanted a Pet Vet Play Set, but I surely didn't want one now!

"Never mind," I said then. "You're right. I don't know what I was thinking coming here." I turned to go.

"Wait!" Kali said, lacing her hands together like she was about to pray and squeezing.

I stopped.

"I want the quilt," Kali admitted, looking pained—like it hurt her to say it.

"Oh." I handed it to her.

Kali held the quilt like it was made of tissue paper.

"Do you want to help me put it on my bed?" she asked.

I shrugged. "Okay."

I followed Kali down a hallway, and when we passed by what must've been the laundry room, I noticed that someone had been ironing—really well. Next to the ironing board was a rolling rack of hanging clothes that looked like they'd come straight from the dry cleaners.

"Is your mom ironing?" I asked.

"No," Kali said, "I am."

I wanted to ask her where she stood on the issue of fitted sheets, but I didn't.

Kali's room was very . . . *white.* The walls and ceiling were white. The furniture was white. The sheets and comforter were white. The whole thing made me think of winter without the hope and warmth of Christmas—January. But resting on her pillow with the kind of faded, matted fur that told me it had been well loved for a long time was a stuffed animal. It was so worn I could barely recognize it as a unicorn—a *unicorn!*

Carefully, Kali removed it from her pillow and placed it on her white nightstand.

I unfolded the quilt as Kali yanked the plain

white comforter off her bed and tossed it aside.

"Where're your parents?" I asked.

"At work," Kali said. "They're *always* at work." She didn't exactly sound happy about that. I decided not to ask any more questions.

As we pulled Grandma Bernice's crazy rainbow-unicorn quilt over Kali's bed, it was like the sun rising over a snow-covered horizon.

While I finished smoothing out my side, I waited. Actually, I'd been waiting the whole time for Kali to say something like, *Oh my gosh! This quilt is so ugly!* But since she hadn't, I risked a quick glance up at her while still smoothing nonexistent wrinkles.

The look on Kali's face, as she stood looking at her bed, told me she loved that quilt. I could see why. It was as if spring had sprung from pure winter with a great big colorful *BOING!* For some reason, I felt glad.

I straightened up and cleared my throat. "Well . . . I guess I'll see you."

I think Kali had somehow forgotten I was there, because she'd been smiling until I spoke. She caught herself and immediately frowned. "This doesn't make us friends," she informed me.

"No, it doesn't," I agreed.

Kali nodded, satisfied. "But I like the quilt, so . . ."

I thought she was going to say, *Thank you.*

But Kali continued, "What do you want for it?"

What did I want for it? I had no idea. Kali tapped the toe of one gleaming white sneaker impatiently.

"I . . . I . . . I don't . . .," I stammered.

"You're *so* weird," Kali said, rolling her eyes. "All you do is stutter and fidget and . . ."

I hate you. That's what I thought Kali was going to say, but she didn't. She didn't say anything. She didn't have to. I knew she hated me. And I knew she'd hated Grandma Bernice. She had said so, repeatedly, to Grandma—my best friend—who was dead! If that wasn't bad enough, now Kali was being mean to me when I'd brought her a gift, a gift made by my best friend, who wouldn't be making any more gifts ever, ever again!

For a minute I was tempted to rip that quilt off Kali's bed and march right out the front door. And that would have been the easiest thing to do, because that's what I wanted to do. That's when I realized that forgiveness isn't an act of weakness. Forgiveness is hard. It takes every ounce of strength and willpower. I trembled from the strain of it. I took deep breaths and tried to calm myself.

Kali rolled her eyes some more.

"I want you to remember Grandma Bernice, Kali," I heard myself say then. "I want you to remember how she forgave you when you told her you hated her. I want you to remember that she was good and kind, even when you were mean to her."

Kali swallowed. "She was nice. I liked Grandma Bernice."

I stood frozen, gaping at her.

Kali continued, "She made me the best sandwich of my life—peanut butter and grape jelly's been my favorite ever since. I make myself one almost every day, but it's never as good as hers was."

"*What?* But you . . . you . . ." I shook my head. It didn't make any sense.

Kali's chin quivered. "I just wished she was *my* Grandma, that she lived with *me*, paid attention to *me*, made *me* cookies and quilts and just . . . loved me to pieces the way she loved you."

I wanted to tell Kali that Grandma had always said that love was the key ingredient in all her food, but I just stood there, fighting the sudden urge to cry. When I got hold of myself, I drew myself up to every centimeter of my full height, just like I'd seen Grandma Bernice do, and I said, "You will never say another cross word about Grandma Bernice ever again."

"No. I won't," Kali said quietly, lowering her head so that I couldn't see her face.

I nodded once and walked out of her room. Halfway down the hall, I heard Kali sobbing. The way she cried somehow told me that her pain was bigger than me, bigger than Grandma Bernice, maybe bigger than any one person or thing. It was a mystery to me how Kali managed to hide all this pain and seem so totally together at school.

But then I remembered the wolves. Kali didn't actually have to have it all together; she just had to *appear* to have it all together, to *appear* be in complete control, and then, most likely, no one would challenge her. But I had. I figured that meant I wasn't the omega wolf anymore. Then, I thought of Alan—my friend—and realized I wasn't a lone wolf either. I'm pretty sure this makes me just a regular wolf—don't you think?

Who Would've Believed?

When I was almost home, I couldn't help noticing the Lanhams' trash, torn up and spread out all over their driveway. The dogs had gotten loose again. I tried to look away and walk on past. But Grandma Bernice's voice echoed somewhere in the back of my mind, "Always leave a place nicer than you found it." I stopped walking and sighed. Ugh!

Piece by piece, I picked up all the trash and put the Lanhams' garbage can back where it belonged, on the side of their house. I didn't enjoy doing it, mind you. It was about as much fun as forgiveness. But still, I did it.

Mrs. Lanham came around her house from the back, wearing yellow rubber gloves up to her elbows. When she saw me putting the lid on her trash can, she looked around and said, "Oh, Lula Bell, thank you, darlin'. I was just coming to clean up that mess."

"That's okay. You're welcome," I said.

"You know, I'm glad to see you. I've been worried about you," Mrs. Lanham said, peeling off her gloves. "I thought I saw you riding your bike over by the cemetery not too long ago. That's awfully far from home."

My toes began to dance.

"But I must've been mistaken," she continued. "You're such a good, smart girl. You'd never do anything that silly and dangerous."

"No, ma'am, I . . . I . . . would—won't. I won't," I managed.

"That's good. Well, thanks again," Mrs. Lanham said, and then she was gone.

I wished that I'd worn rubber gloves. My hands were so grimy and sticky, I thought I'd best not touch anything, like our doorknob. So, I went around to the back of our house to wash my hands with the garden hose.

"I knew you could do it," I heard Mama's voice say as I turned the water spigot off.

I stood, looked around, and found her sitting in a rocking chair on our back porch. I had to think for a second, but then I remembered: the talent show. I nodded.

I wiped my hands on my jeans and came to sit in the rocker beside Mama's. "Did you see Great Uncle Cleburne? Is he okay?"

Mama pressed her lips together and shook her head. A wave of golden hair fell across her face.

"Did he die?" I whispered.

"Yes, late last night," Mama said, pushing her hair back. She looked tired—not mad-tired but tired-tired.

"I'm sorry, Mama."

She nodded as she stared off into the distance. "I'm just glad I was there when Uncle Cleburne went. Thank you for that, Lula Bell. I'm just *so* glad."

"You are?" I said, because I found that hard to believe. Being there when someone dies had to be scary, I thought.

Mama stopped rocking and turned to look me in the eyes. Her face was serious. "Honey, if I hadn't been there, I would've missed one of the most precious moments of my life."

I nodded like I understood, even though I didn't.

But Mama continued to stare at me.

I looked away.

"Look at me, Lula Bell."

I did as I was told.

"I want you to know that Uncle Cleburne closed his eyes and smiled. Then he said, 'I see her! I see Bernice! She has doughnuts! She says she's waiting for me!' And then he went. Uncle Cleburne went with a big smile on his face."

I didn't say anything, just sat there, trying to take this in.

Mama must've taken this to mean that I didn't believe her, because after a few minutes she said, "One of the nurses told me that dying people often hallucinate, due to a lack of oxygen in the brain . . . but . . . well . . ." Mama shrugged her shoulders and started rocking again.

I started rocking, too.

After a good long while, I smiled. "Grandma Bernice died happy, too, Mama. On our last Thursday night together, she told me that what she really and truly wanted was to die peacefully in her sleep, having been surrounded by people she loved."

Mama didn't react at all. I wasn't even sure she'd heard me.

"She even died on the day she wanted," I whispered.

Mama stopped rocking and looked at me. "She wanted to die on her birthday?"

"Yes, ma'am. Grandma said she thought it was nice when a person died on the same day they were born. She said it gave the impression that things went exactly as planned—she called it 'elegant.'"

Mama threw back her head and laughed in spite of herself. She looked almost exactly like she did in the photo on Grandma Bernice's nightstand.

For a good while after that, Mama and I just sat, thinking and rocking together in a comfortable kind of silence.

Finally, Mama stopped rocking and said, "We'll see Grandma again, Lula Bell. We're just going to go a little longer in between visits is all. In the meantime, I know she's happy, and she wants us to be happy, too."

I nodded.

Mama stood. "I've got to start thinking about supper."

"I'm going to stay out here a little longer," I said, "if that's all right."

"Whatever makes you happy," Mama said, winking at me as she disappeared into the house and closed the door behind her.

At first, I only heard it: the unmistakable vibrating sound of tiny wings that beat somewhere between forty and eighty times per second. Then, hovering in the air, near Grandma Bernice's lilacs, I swear I saw it: a solid white hummingbird!

"Let's go out for supper tonight," Daddy was saying to Mama when I went inside.

Mama and I both looked at the chicken thawing on the kitchen counter.

Then, an amazing thing happened: Mama picked up the chicken and put it back in the refrigerator.

An Announcement

I was kind of cranky that night at the Mexican restaurant because our server brought my drink in a kiddie cup—insulting! (If you are a server in a restaurant, here's a little tip for you: assume that any kid who walks pretty good and doesn't drool knows how to drink from a glass just fine. Hmph!)

Anyway, over fajitas, Mama had an announcement to make: "I've decided to sell the beauty shop."

"That's good. How'd you finally decide?" Daddy said, setting his glass back down on the table.

Mama shook her head. "You'll think I'm nuts."

"I won't think that. I've *known* it for years," Daddy teased.

Mama smiled. Then she leaned over the table and whispered to both of us, "I asked Grandma Bernice what I should do."

Daddy narrowed his eyes at Mama. "And she answered you?"

Mama nodded, sat back, and started fishing through her gigantic purse. Daddy looked over at me. He looked just a teensy bit worried.

Mama handed Daddy a piece of paper. He read it and smiled at Mama.

"What?" I said, feeling left out. "What? What is it?"

Ignoring me, Mama said to Daddy, "I was looking for the tape when I came across that letter in a drawer. It was the only letter—I don't even know how it got there."

"WHAT?" I said a little too loudly. People at other tables turned to look.

"Please excuse us," Mama said to the other people.

When the other people went back to their suppers, Mama answered me. "It's a letter Grandma Bernice wrote to me eight years ago, before she moved in with us, back when I first opened the beauty shop."

Daddy read aloud from the letter: "I know your new beauty parlor will bring you much success and happiness. Just remember that time goes by far too quickly. Don't forget to watch as Lula Bell grows and begins to make her way in the world."

"So?" I said.

"So, Grandma Bernice was absolutely right," Mama said. "That was the answer I'd been looking for, the one I needed to make my decision."

"So you're just going to stay home and watch me grow *all the time?*" I said. "Because I'm pretty sure you can't *actually* see it happening."

"I can see it," Mama said, smiling.

Being Uniquely U

The bad news is that the rest of May and all of June were gone before I knew it. Mama put me to work right alongside her, from morning 'til night—and I hadn't even complained or anything! But it was like the ironing, I guess: Mama really needed the help. Since she helps me so much, I figure I have to help her right back. (Although, I admit I've stopped ironing the sheets. Who notices wrinkles when they're sleeping?)

The good news is that the house doesn't seem so sad and empty anymore. Maybe that's because it isn't. Mama's customers are in and out all day every day, having their hair done in our garage, pouring themselves sweet tea in our kitchen, and gossiping to anybody, anywhere, who'll listen. Nobody says anything truly mean. Well, okay, occasionally they say mean*ish* things, but whenever that happens, they bless the person they said mean things about right away. Like yesterday, when Mrs. Hubbs said, "Have y'all seen Lily Kate Cohen's new hairdo?" And then Mrs. Brubaker said, "Oh yes, honey. Isn't it the awfulest thing you ever saw? God bless her!"

"Yes, God bless her," Mama repeated, "and God bless her hair stylist, who is *not* me—I just want y'all to know that." (Here's a little tip for you: apparently, you can get away with saying almost anything about anybody, so long as you follow it with a God-bless-her or -him. Watch this: "That guy is a total idiot! God bless him." Works pretty good, huh?)

Well, anyway, Mama turned our garage into a small beauty shop, and there is now a sign on the door that reads "Uniquely U Salon." I hate the sign and the name—isn't it terrible?—but when I tried to tell Mama so, she said, "It's a unique name for a unique salon that encourages its clients to be uniquely themselves."

"I don't even know what that's supposed to mean," I said.

Mama said, "Women waste too much time trying to be someone else. If they have straight hair, they want curly hair; if they have curly hair, they want straight hair; if they're brunettes, they want to be blondes. Whatever they haven't got, that's what they want."

I thought about this and then said, "Um, I don't mean to be rude or anything, but . . . isn't that kind of your job?"

"Not anymore," Mama said. "Now, I try to call my clients' attention to what they *do* have instead of what they don't and to make the best of it."

I knew instantly that this meant I'd need a different hair stylist when I grew up, since I definitely plan to be curly-haired and blond.

There is a sign inside the salon that I like, though. It says "The higher your hair is, the closer you are to heaven." Celia Thompson likes that one, too. She comes over to have her hair done by Mama sometimes. Other times, Celia just comes over to tap dance and sing with me.

Emilou Meriweather comes over sometimes, too. We get along so good and have so much fun together that several times, I've been tempted to ask

Emilou why we ever stopped being friends—why, exactly, *she* stopped being *my* friend. But I never have. I never will. There are three reasons for this:

1) Emilou probably decided she didn't want to be my friend for the same kinds of reasons that I once decided I didn't want to be Alan West's friend. So I was no better, no different than Emilou. We'd both made a mistake. Actually, I'd made lots of mistakes.

2) Even so, Alan never once asked me to explain exactly why I'd done all the things I'd done, which was a good thing, because that would've been really embarrassing. Since Alan didn't ask me, I figured I didn't have any right to ask Emilou.

3) I didn't want to make Emilou feel uncomfortable or embarrassed. I like her, and I like her karaoke machine, which she always brings with her when she comes over.

Daddy says that Emilou, Celia, and I are all bright, shining stars. (Luckily, we haven't had any problems with mobs of adoring fans or paparazzi—yet.)

Daddy still calls every night that he's away from home, only now Mama and I both talk to him every single night.

Even breakfast has turned out to be okay. Mama still serves me cold cereal, but there are lots of prizes. Why, just yesterday morning I won a Mega-Map of the United States! When I told Daddy, he said that before he left home next time, he'd stick thumbtacks in all the places he'd be performing so that I'd know exactly where he was in the world on any given day.

Mama still serves cookies from a box, too, although on special occasions, we have Krispy Kreme doughnuts. Both are better than a life without cookies or doughnuts altogether.

Oh yeah, and Alan West comes over with his camera every afternoon and sits on the back porch, waiting for that white hummingbird to come back.

This afternoon, I said, "But, Alan, what if it never comes back?"

"It'll come back," Alan said, "and I'll be here when it does. I'm a very patient person."

"I know," I said, "but what if it doesn't?"

"It will," Alan insisted. Then he smiled. "And when I prove the existence of the albino humming-bird, just think how it'll look on my permanent record!"

"Faith is the substance of things hoped for," I muttered.

"That's right," Alan said.

We went back to watching the regular hum-mingbirds zipping around the feeders that Alan had put up in Grandma Bernice's garden. Oh, we had plenty of hummingbirds all right. They just weren't white.

"Alan?" I said quietly.

"Yes?" he said without looking at me. He was still too busy watching his feeders.

"Do you think there's any chance at all that the white hummingbird could be Grandma Bernice?"

"Like reincarnation?" Alan said.

I nodded.

Alan didn't answer me right away. After a few minutes, he began reciting:

"Do not stand at my grave and weep,
I am not there; I do not sleep.

I am a thousand winds that blow,
I am the diamond glints on snow—"

I covered my face with both hands and groaned, "Not this again!"

"Lula Bell, I memorized the whole thing!" Alan said, grinning, as he continued:

"I am the sun on ripened grain,
I am the gentle autumn rain.
When you awaken in the morning's hush
I am the swift uplifting rush
of quiet birds in circled flight.
I am the soft starlight at night.
Do not stand at my grave and cry,
I am not there; I did not die."

I gave Alan an exasperated sigh. "So you think it's possible," I said, just to be clear.

"Anything's possible, Lula Bell. It's possible that we'll see an albino hummingbird today, when no one knows if they even exist."

"You're my best friend, Alan," I said—quick—before before I lost my courage.

Alan smiled a huge smile then, like he'd just

snapped the picture that would prove the existence of the albino hummingbird for his permanent record.

"You're my best friend, too, Lula Bell."

I'm beginning to think that maybe there's no such thing as freaks and geeks. Maybe we're all just people looking for our people, our friends, our place of belonging. Now that I've found mine, I don't feel freaky or geeky at all, even though I'm still the same freak/geek girl I was to begin with. So . . . hmmm. I'll have to think on that some more.

Anyway, after Alan went home, I went inside and found Mama pouring herself some sweet tea. She took a sip, then set the glass down on the counter and said, "You know, that Alan, he's going to be a real heartbreaker one day."

"You're just saying that because of his hair," I said.

Mama had cut Alan's hair, and I have to admit it looked great—nowhere near disastrous. In fact, Alan West was almost cute.

"It's a good haircut. The trick is a dry cut, not too long and not too short," Mama said. "But he's a good lookin' boy . . . and just wait 'til the girls find out he reads poetry!"

"Were you *spying* on us?" I shrieked. "I knew it! I knew it was going to be like this when you decided to stay home and watch me grow!"

Mama laughed. "What's the matter with you? Why are you so mad all of a sudden?"

I didn't know why. So I said, "I'm not mad; I'm just tired is all."

"Well, you better rest up. The Purdys' Fourth of July picnic is tomorrow."

Fainting goats! I could hardly wait!

Acknowledgments:

First and foremost, I thank God, who's brought me this far—which couldn't have been easy, since I tend to get lost—a lot. Fortunately, there were many bright, guiding lights posted along the way, and I am grateful for each and every one of them:

Thanks to my entire family, many of whom are gifted storytellers, but all of whom have enriched my life beyond measure.

Special thanks to my mother, Ann, my father, David, and my stepmother, Janet, who still save all their best stories and favorite books to share with me, as they have for the past thirty years.

Unending gratitude to my husband, Mark, who was there for every rejection letter, administering the necessary dosages of junk food, after which he dusted the crumbs off me, wiped my tears, and somehow talked me into giving more when I felt like giving up. I truly have no idea who I might be without Mark; I only know that I would be someone lesser than I am.

Thanks to my girls, Laurel Grace and Erin Christine, whose love and light shine as bright as the sun. Without them, I wouldn't know which direction to reach and bend and grow.

Thanks to my sister, Sarah Clark, who read and reread this manuscript (she's a writer's writer), who's always there to help, and who generally makes me feel less crazy—this is no small thing!

Thanks to my sister, Leslie R. Smith, who flat-out tells me when I'm being crazy. Her wise counsel has altered my life's course many times, and I am a better, stronger, happier person for it.

Thanks to my friend, Richard Smith Mize, who also altered my life's course in the best possible way: by believing in me.

Thanks to the public school system of Kentucky, through which I encountered several more bright lights in the form of teachers: Lisa Saylor, Betty Larson, Martha Browning, and Marian Sims.

For inspiration, I must thank:

the real Grandma Bernice Payne, who loved 'mater sandwiches, welcomed one and all to her table, fed us well, and made us laugh;

Joseph E. Stopher, who loved lobster soup and

never missed Sunday school—or anything else that was important to him;

Marie E. Stopher, who made everything possible for Joe, and who also happens to have the most beautiful head of wavy white hair I've ever seen;

Roy Lanphear, a WWII veteran with a wonderfully wicked sense of humor, who always sang as he went about his work and loved to talk politics . . .

. . . until Ruth Lanphear determined that politics were bad for Roy's heart. Ruth was a superb storyteller, doughnut maker, and quilter—and I still miss her.

As always, a million thanks to my cold readers: Sydney Hurt and Joyce Payne. They kept me going.

Even so, this particular book would've never been published without additional help from a number of people:

My father, David—the best, most brilliant writer I know—thought this manuscript was salvageable when I did not. More important, he told me how to salvage it. I took his advice and exploited his ideas shamelessly. He saw me—and this book—through many long, dark nights.

When morning came, author/editor Kara LaReau was there to lend a hand.

It is thanks to Kara's unwavering belief in Lula Bell that literary agent Emily van Beek soon joined Team Lula Bell. Emily and I took turns sitting with Lula Bell, holding her hand, encouraging her, and loving her all the while. Then, when she finally seemed strong enough, Emily placed Lula Bell in just the right hands.

The most capable hands I can imagine for a novel are those of my editor, Melanie Kroupa. It is thanks to her editorial guidance, in addition to the help and hard work of all the other tremendously talented folks at Marshall Cavendish, that this book—finally!—found its way home to you. I will always be grateful.

Finally, I wish to thank two very special readers, Alaine Carpenter and Jennifer Owen, both merry, marvelous librarians—and now friends—who stepped right up to claim me as their own. Their libraries will always feel like home.